The SHUTTERED HOUSES of PARIS

The SHUTTERED HOUSES of PARIS

Being a Companion Volume
to the
"Pretty Women of Paris"

*Printed for Private Circulation
in a limited Edition of One Hundred and
Fifty Copies only.*
1906

BLUE MOON BOOKS
NEW YORK

Published by
Blue Moon Books
841 Broadway, Fourth Floor
New York, NY 10003

ISBN 1-56201-152-9

Manufactured in the United States of America

PUBLISHER'S NOTE

The history of erotic literature is long and distinguished. It holds valuable lessons and insights for the general reader, the sociologist, the student of sexual behavior, and the literary specialist interested in knowing how people of different cultures and different times acted and how these actions relate to the present.

Because of the inherent value to all students of the human condition of these classic erotic works, we have chosen not to alter this book in any way, shape, or form. It is presented to the reader exactly as it first appeared in print. Thus, all of the subtleties are exposed to our view—the haste or extreme care taken by the author and the original publisher, the manner of speech and communication, the colloquialisms of the time, the means of expression, and the concepts of erotic stimulation—both real and imaginary—used by the writer who was, in every sense, representative of his time.

"From the lips ever-living of laughter and love everlasting,
that leave

In the cleft of his heart who shall kiss them a snake to
'corrode it and cleave."

SWINBURNE.

"One that was a woman, sir; but, rest her soul, she's dead."

SHAKESPEARE.

"Women are ever in extremes; they are either better or
worse than men."

LA BRUYERE.

CONTENTS

CHAPTER I.

Which is a Preface in Disguise 5

CHAPTER II.

No. 14, Rue Montyon. 24

CHAPTER III.

Rue de Londres. 48

CHAPTER IV.

The Assignation Houses of the Etoile Quarter. . 64

CHAPTER V.

How Venus is Worshipped in the La Villette and
  La Chapelle District.   A Trip from Rue Bur-
  nouf to Rue Jolivet, with Some Account of a
  Mystery of Montparnasse. 98

CHAPTER VI.

The Brothel of La Farcie: No. 4, Rue Joubert. 144

CHAPTER VII.

Round About the Bibliotheque Nationale and the
Bourse 155

CHAPTER VIII.

The Temple of the Rue Taitbout 179

CHAPTER IX.

From the Gare de l'Est to the Big Boulevards . . 190

CHAPTER X.

The Rue Laferriere, with a Few Words about
the Flagellants of the Rue Clauzel . . . 201

CHAPTER XI.

Mélanie, the Man-Tamer 227

CHAPTER XII.

Student's Brothels 239

CHAPTER XIII.

Round the Halles 256

CHAPITRE XIV.

At Grenelle 264

CHAPITRE XV.

A Common-Error. — "Lookers-On." — Socratic
Love 273

The Shuttered Houses of Paris

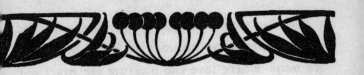

CHAPTER I.

Which is a Preface in Disguise.

Reader friend, a word with you, I pray.

Paris is the home of the gods in a land of laughter. But how many Parisians are there who have thoroughly explored their own city? Setting apart places of amusement whose diversions are publicly announced in the daily papers, the citizens of the French capital know naught of all those joys which form the principal charm of life.

The proof of what I dare to set forth here is furnished by the mistaken reply of that gracious patrician lady who, listening to the cry of a blind beggar : " Pity a poor man who is deprived of the greatest charm of life ! " remarked : " Is he an eunuch ? "

On the surface of the globe there may be towns quite as voluptuous as Paris, but there are none where love and pleasure are practised with more exquisite refinement. Professional Venuses hurry to the banks of the Seine from the four quarters of the world, and bringing their science with them, form apprentices of passion who, in their turn, pass on the knowledge of sense-exacerbation to others and so the pretty women of the City of Light are skilled in every branch of venery.

Why then travel in search of sexual pleasure?

First and foremost, we have Montmartre. There you will find charmers of the Arab, Spanish, and Hungarian types, living and breathing portraits of the beauties of those countries. They have inherited the best points of sturdy visitors from these lands, who have imprinted their racial peculiarities upon the greedy and receptive wombs of the sweet Parisiennes of our outlying districts.

My reader may question the necessity of so much circumlocution when merely about to speak of prostitution, which, please make no mistake, is a highly moral subject. Grave scientists have discussed the question. Masters of social economy, doctors and philanthropists have grown grey in the study of the social evil and have blushed with rapture whenever they lighted upon some new stupid error, dubbed a great discovery.

Where does prostitution begin and where does it finish?

I elude the query. This book has been a labour of love. I would that you had as much pleasure in running through its pages as I experienced while composing it. I leave the moral aspect of the picture to wiser hands and brains than mine.

In ancient Greece, prostitutes formed three distinct classes—the hetairas, the flute-players, and those who sat patiently waiting for hire in houses of ill-fame.

The hetairas were courtesans of the highest rank, such as Aspasia, to whom Demosthenes replied, after having enquired the price of her favours : " I do not buy repentance so dearly ! "

Since the fall of the Second Empire there are no more hetairas in France. The last was Madame de Païva, who began life as a flower-girl in the street. After a checquered career, she became the lawful wife of M. de Païva, and died mistress of Count Henckel von Donners-marck, a noble Prussian officer, who was governor of Strasburg during the Franco-Prussian war of 1870-71. He built his concubine a splendid palace in the Avenue des Champs-Elysées, which after his death, became a restaurant, and is now occupied by the Paris branch of the London Travellers' Club. The monogram and crown of the original owner can still be made out in the arabesques of the front railings.

The flute-playing females of Paris are generally in very comfortable circumstances, but some are much poorer, who, with a neat skirt and blouse, worth perhaps a louis in all, are as delightfully tempting in their cheap and tasteful get-up as if they were dressed in Paquin's latest masterpieces.

Let us halt here a moment and enjoy a slight

digression. We will suppose we are on the racecourse of Longchamps, or enjoying our dinner in the gorgeous saloons of the Hotel Ritz; taking tea at Rumpelmayer's, or chuckling over a naughty comedy at the theatre. At all these places we meet with delicious *cocottes*— the tip-top tarts of Paris.

Every one of these venal sirens, with hungry eye and greedy grasp, has had to pass through several stages of apprenticeship before being able to parade in the fashionable front of the battle of life, with a dress from Doucet's and a hat designed by Lewis. If you are an early riser, stroll up the Faubourg du Temple at eight o'clock in the morning, or else walk down the same thoroughfare at eight in the evening. See the streams of pretty workgirls. Are they not winsome, and fresh as rosebuds just gathered? Their hats are rakishly perched on their undyed tresses, and they look at every likely male with an arch glance, as if defying him to try a fall in Cupid's arena. They earn fifteen-pence a day, and work their fingers to the bone. But they dream of other things. Each has a little love-affair to fill the vacant space in her heart. The chosen sweetheart is a lad of their own age who also has visions of easily-earned gold, and he relies on the charms of his girl to realise his ambitious longings.

Thus advised by her cynical lover, the young lass makes her way over the bridges to the Latin Quarter, among the students. If you run across such a tender morsel of feminity and she attracts you, tell her so boldly. For a five-franc piece, you can have your will of her.

A short time passes and already the saucy minx has lost much of her pristine girlish grace. She then returns to the fashionable side of the silver Seine and you may meet her with a little bundle or bonnet-box. She looks like a milliner's apprentice. Or else, she walks out dressed up to the nines, generally in bad taste, unsuited to the season, or the weather at that moment. She is to be met with under the arcades of the Rue de Rivoli, or in the Rue de la Paix. Nightfall finds her in the vicinity of the Saint Lazare railway station. If you hunger for her now, she will cost you ten francs. When she grows into precocious womanhood, the healthy colour of a damsel in her teens fading away, she frequents the lounge of some variety palace and inaugurates a higher scale of prices, except when hard-up. Then she is more accommodating and the scantiest purse may command her caresses. If she is lucky enough to conquer some unsophisticated young bachelor with lots of cash, no one can hold her. In that case, her glory is without limits. She finds herself quickly at the head of a sumptuous household, with an automobile, pearl necklace, diamonds, furs, lace, and carriages and horses.

Such is the simple story of our precious cocottes; the naked scoffolding of a modern harlot's progress in the gayest of cities. When our scarlet ladies were young and pretty; while the bloom was on their peach-like cheeks, a five-franc piece was their maximum. Now that all trace of their virginal beauty has given place to powder and peroxide, for a night in their lace-trimmed sheets they ask and get the year's wage of an average skilled artisan. The gilt frame has to be paid for, not the picture. The scenery commands the gold, not the actress. Costly dresses, servants' wages, interest on other fellows' gifts of jewellery—all this has to be settled. Numerous lovers are glad to write out cheques. They do so readily, for the woman is now a fashionable perfumed idol, and to be in the fashion yourself, you must sleep with expensive, worn-out, painted ladies.

Snobs and snobbery are universal, to be found everywhere—even in the bidet-bath and injection apparatus of the light o' love.

These high-class haughty beauties are mostly sought after by vainglorious swells, quite a common type in Paris. They pay a woman vast sums of money merely for the honour of being seen in her company, when she must be dressed six months in advance of the fashions and be blazing with precious stones. Real male martyrs to the gnawing manias of sensuality hide all trace of their sins and seek out these mercenary courtesans on the sly, wishing to enjoy their charms in the secret silence of their sumptuous bedrooms, and are scarcely ever seen speaking to the adored angel in public.

The second class of prostitutes in Greece were the flute-payers. The discreet allusion can be readily fathomed, and we may apply it to our red-lipped sirens without fear of contradiction. But in ancient times these girls were really musicians. Nowadays, a modern Hamlet would thus address the Gallic demireps, as they smiled upon him with meretricious, moist mouths : " Can'st thou play upon this pipe ? 'Tis as easy as lying down ! "

In our time, if there are no professional beauties who make a living out of real music, there are still numerous sprightly fairies who go on the stages of theatres or music-halls for the sake of parading their shapely limbs under the limelight and so increasing the circle of their friends and customers. Mademoiselle Emilienne d'Alencon paid a goodly sum for some trained rabbits and exhibited them in a circus a few years ago, and Madame " Bob " Walter worked hard to outrival the world-renowned Loïe Fuller in her serpentine dances. Madame Liane de Pougy shines on the boards as a pet of the ballet in London as well as in Paris, and the Spanish strumpet, beautiful Otéro, adopts the same tactics.

By such exhibitions, half-naked behind the footlights, the woman of pleasure acquires that indispensable advertisement and notoriety which enable her to quote fantastic figures before she deigns to open her arms—and legs. Scanty stage costume and scenic illusion enhance her beauty and increase her allurement tenfold. Many of the richest woman-hunters who, in a crowd, would pass the prettiest girl in the world with indifference, feel their sign of manhood vigorously stirring when they notice how hundreds of opera glasses are aimed at a grease-painted chorus girl, showing her thighs in silk tights; three quarters of her bosom; and the bushes of her armpits to the gloating occupants of stalls and boxes. We can therefore understand why clever and cultured men of the world have lavished gold upon ugly old women who, thanks to the artifices of the theatre, pass muster when the curtain draws up.

I know an actress of small comedy parts, who without a hair on her head or a tooth in her jaws, is kept in magnificent style, and lives in a mansion, now belonging to her, near the Etoile triumphal arch.

As I have already said, it is not necessary that this class of ladies should be actresses or possess a knowledge of music.

If there exist a number of rich gentlemen with a desire to buy only the best, most widely-advertised, and fashionable goods in the market; who will only have to do with notable cocottes; there are, on the other hand, many who are actuated by a secret Puritanical feeling of respectability. Such amateurs open their purses without stint when the woman they want is not a known unfortunate.

This explains why some girls stick to a trade although subsidised by a wealthy lover, and carry on some light business. In their early youth they have mostly been living lay-figures at male dressmaker's establishments, artificial flower-makers, or they may have graduated as milliners or seamstresses. To appreciate the grace of the natty bodice-fitters and skirt hands of the gay city, you have but to linger in the Rue de la Paix when these fairies troop in shoals to business in the morning, wander on the neighbouring Boulevards during their luncheon hour, or flutter into the dark streets when the day's work is done.

Between nine and ten o'clock in the morning the nymphs of the needle hurry to their workshops. If she is invited out to dinner, the workgirl gets away at seven in the evening, or an hour later when forced to put up with the indifferent food doled out to her by her firm. The best way to pick up a naughty minx with a roughened forefinger is to play the early bird. At night, your Don-Juan-like endeavours will be in vain. Someone is waiting at a neighbouring *café*, a street corner, or ensconced in a handy omnibus or tramway office. At dusk, these sewing maids will not listen to you, nor is there any hope for the next day. With the lack of foresight peculiar to youth, having arranged their nocturnal pastimes, they cannot trouble about a fresh suitor. Unless, of course, growing cynically and lustfully desperate, you pull out a well-lined pocket book, proving that you are prepared to offer irresistible arguments.

The street-walkers, to be found in all the best and most populous parts of Paris, may likewise be catalogued in the second division.

I now come to the third and last class : the boarders in the brothels.

The aim of my volume is to study the manners and customs of the principal public harems, not forgetting minor temples of love and vice.

I have just given a rapid review of the priestesses of Venus who pass up and down the rungs of the ladder of social lust in the capital of France.

The police regulations concerning prostitution have, rightly or wrongly, refused to accept any classification ressembling that of antiquity. The French authorities divide prostitution into two categories : *filles soumises*—registered women—and *filles clandestines*—who sell themselves without being pigeon-holed by the guardians of law and order. These guerilla girls are hunted down relentlessly, while the powers that be show great respect for kept women who live in good style.

The poor registered creatures are subdivided by the police as *filles-éparses*—scattered prostitutes — and *filles en carte* — bawdy - house wenches.

All have to undergo a medical examination by the police doctor, and submit to the speculum at the head-office on certain fixed dates. If they are granted a clean bill of health, their card of registration is stamped accordingly. If found to be contaminated or unfit for public service, they are sent to the hospital.

In this respect, of course, the woman of the shuttered house offers more sanitary security than the scattered prostitute, as the brothel-keeper takes good care that his girls submit regularly to the government ordeal of inspection. Otherwise, he is liable to be punished, according to the bye-laws regulating his license. The free demirep, either out of laziness or sheer neglect, laughs at fine or imprisonment, and only hearkens to the prompting of her wayward spirit. If she lets the day of medical investigation slip by, all she does is to change her lodgings and choose fresh haunts. Has she been in the habit of soliciting on the Boulevard Sébastopol, she will go to work at the top of the Avenue des Champs-Elysées, among the grooms, coachmen, and upper servants of the aristocratic Etoile quarter.

Formerly, houses of official prostitution were recognisable by the characteristic appearance of their frontage, with green shutters always kept closed in front of every window, and the big number over the door, painted on ground glass, becoming luminous to catch the eye of the passer-by suggestively at night.

For several generations, these gigantic figures were strictly ordered by the police authorities, but lately they seem to think that this outward and visible sign of " debauchery supplied " has something decidedly immoral about it.

So the large numerals have disappeared, and all that remains in Paris is a transparency of normal size where the number of the house gleams in the darkness, to show that the hospitable abbess, with her crew of cloistered living dolls has lit up the beacon of ready-made voluptuousness.

It is not needful to describe every bagnio in Paris, but after having minutely depicted the best seraglios, where really pretty, well-made, naked, complaisant young women are to be found, I will throw a cursory glance at some typical retreats, as well as sketching a few minor, unpretending stews—all as I saw them with my own eyes.

My aim is to conscientiously study the inmates of the first-rate accommodation houses of Paris. For that reason, I shall say no more about kept women and other free-lances of higher circles.

Perhaps one day, in another volume, I may try to paint a picture of the scattered waifs of the pleasure-loving city, and divulge the secrets of clandestine, unlicensed, hole and corner prostitution.

The field is a vast one and full of palpitating

interest. Who knows, for instance, anything about what goes on in a street of the La Villette district, called the Rue Burnouf, which winds in and out, cut here and there by steep flights of stone steps? In this alley, hideous hags offer their vile expert services for a few coppers. Among the shrubs of the Tuileries gardens, skirting the Rue des Pyramides, or in the Champs-Elysées, near the Marigny theatre, shadowy creatures accost hurrying pedestrians in the dark. There are a goodly number of *al fresco* clients, without counting male accomplices, and children who accompany the old witches. These public gardens are frequented by a peculiar set of erotomaniacs—*voyeurs*, or " lookers-on. " They pay these pariah prostitutes small amounts on condition that the miserable females allow them to watch customers being masturbated or enjoying hasty emission in any other way. Sometimes the nymph of the night offers herself gratis to a passer-by if he will only let the " looker-on " glut his eyes with their sports. All such strange agreements ofttimes lead to quarrels and scenes of violence which cause the police to intervene.

At the Salle Wagram dancing-hall, and in the Bullier ball-room of the Latin Quarter, the pederastic youths of Paris—the monarchs of masculine prostitution—hold their court once a year on Shrove Tuesday, when, profiting by the licence of Carnival misrule, they are able to dress openly as women and hide their polluted sex in skirts and petticoats.

It is a strange sight, from a physiological and psychological standpoint, to see these good-looking lads, most carefully painted, perfumed and frocked, mincing and coquetting with effeminate affected airs and graces.

Such extraordinary perversity is noteworthy and deserves the fullest attention which I may devote to it at some period in the near future. Throughout these pages, I will not dive too deeply into the slough of hireling sensuality, but skim instead over the surface, embracing a wider expanse.

I hope to be of service to inquisitive readers desirous of becoming acquainted with details of how women live and love in the brothels of Paris.

I will try and show the observe and reverse of this meretricious medal, but not with the preconceived ideas of a narrow-minded, austere moralist, who without a word of pity for the weaknesses and exigencies of poor humanity, paints everything with colours of most sombre hue. Judging facts impartially, aiming at scrupulous truthfulness, you will witness with me the whirlings of the merry-go-round of fast life between four walls, and I will set down in plain language all we see.

It is my hope that in the following chapters, my readers will find food for earnest thought, as well as entertainment; approving my efforts by being indulgent enough to forgive the faults and errors of a most humble searcher for light in the bye-ways of masculine lechery and venal female frailty.

CHAPTER II.

No. 14, Rue Montyon.

———

Baron de Montyon was a philanthropist who died in 1820, and bequeathed three millions of francs to hospital charities, besides founding yearly prizes for virtuous folks. Every twelve months the French Academy distributes these pecuniary encouragements for honesty and purity, endowing virgins with the good man's gold. A street is named after him in Paris. In that thoroughfare stands one of the best, if not the handsomest brothel in the capital. Strange irony of fate !

This temple of vice, standing cynically in the street of virtue, is sumptuously decorated. All is, however, in good taste. Artists have decorated and upholstered each room, and although minutely garnishing every corner, they have not forgotten the general effect.

The most fastidious taste in house-furnishing can be gratified in this confortable establishment. If you are of a classical turn of mind, stirred into admiration at a reminiscence of antique Greece in the days of Pericles, you may sacrifice on the altar of love in a bed-chamber of the purest Greek style, arranged from authentic architectural authorities.

Another cosy nook shows us boldly-sculptured cariatides in a Renaissance room, where proud and beautiful Imperia would be quite at home, if by a miracle the enchantress who bewitched Popes and cardinals could once more return to our worn-out ball of clay. It is perhaps better that she remain unconscious in the silence of her restful tomb, for should she come back among us mortals, the handsome sensual witch would suffer more atrocious torture than she can possibly endure in the hottest corner of purgatory, where, if we listen to priestly chronicles, she is still broiling—was she not a whore? Her torments on earth would arise from the pangs of jealousy, as she would see in this accessible harem lovely women worthy of standing naked beside her—the siren whose reputation for beauty still lives through the ages—and this comparison of fleshly perfection and grace might tend to her confusion and to the advantage of the pets of Paris.

I speak advisedly, for despite the incredulous mocking smiles of my readers, I can assure my brethren in debauchery that real Lutetian lasses, born within the circle of the fortifications, are to be seen and fully enjoyed in the mansion of the Rue Montyon.

I enter, and find myself in a reception room of perfectly correct Louis XV. style, with the addition of every modern refinement of necessity, including electric lights which gleam in every nook. Electricity, that capricious modern force, is even used to set the piano playing all by itself; the motor being carefully hidden.

Near the mechanical instrument stands a young woman—a splendid specimen of feminine beauty. She wears a blue peplum, and in an attitude of superb immodesty has thrown her light robe wide open. As I gaze admiringly at her, she continues to push the folds of her single scanty garment behind her back. Thanks to her accommodating gestures, I am able to view the well-nigh perfect scaffolding of her magnificent body ; her noble, shapely legs, encased in embroidered, grey silk stockings ; her white polished belly, where blossoms that mysterious hairy tuft, the dark fleece shading her mark of sex ; the breasts, stiffly crowned with their two pink points ; and her insolent posteriors seem to jut out more audaciously, so to speak, beneath the touch of her tapering fingers drawing aside her drapery. Her features are small and pretty, and her little head is carried proudly and seducingly on a long, smooth, rounded neck. She has the profile of a Roman maid. Every one of her postures is naturally graceful, enhanced by the slow, almost scientifically-calculated play of her voluptuously-moulded arms. As she stands thus to welcome my friends and myself—a cheerful set of club-men—she seems as if defying a painter's or a sculptor's criticism, posing without effort as the model of a really handsome girl.

We ask her name, and she replies: "Carmen!" Her voice is sweetly penetrating, with an echo as clear as crystal, still vibrating, even when her pulpy mouth closes after she has spoken. She smiles, and as her crimson lips open slightly, her white teeth are shown, and a tremor of desire ripples over our flesh.

" If you will allow me, Carmen, you shall be my queen this night ! "

The beautiful damsel come near to us, and offers me her mouth—a calyx that is fresh despite its warmth, and as her kiss skims over my moustache, her inquisitive fingers seek at once to find out whether I am prepared for the delicious combat of copulation.

My charmer is not disappointed. I am ready, and should have no difficult task to perform. I have only to place myself in the proper position and press my rigid spear into the sheath provided by Nature.

That decisive moment has not yet arrived. It is more prudent to curb my unreasoning impatience. The rummaging curiosity of Carmen's investigating hand may bring about a catastrophe.

" No, no! Not like that! Let me be! " I remonstrate involuntarily. "

" Why ? "

" By and by. Let us open a few bottles of champagne first. These gentlemen, my friends, whom I have conducted here, would like to see some of the pretty sights of your house. "

Carmen claps her hands joyfully together.

" Am I to be one of the party ? "

" Certainly. Haven't you got a particular little comrade to introduce to us ? "

" Of course ! I have indeed a pet chum. Come here, Suzanne ! "

A petite, fair wench, as plump as an ortolan, with dimples in her arms, cheeks and posterior globes ; an incarnation of merry, laughing porcelain roguery, approaches trippingly.

We choose some other tender females. There are three men forming our party, in all, but we mean to employ four women. This combination is the lowest number granted to visitors, when it is intended to form living pictures worthy of the admiration of delicate refined rakes.

The discreet and affable housekeeper brings the sparkling juice of the grape, pours the foaming wine into the glasses, and carries the silver tray round the room. All the ladies take a sip and get to work without further loss of time.

Their dressing-gowns of silk and lace, ajar from neck to foot, are thrown widely open, and form a pleasing background to the pearly brilliancy of their pink flesh, of which we can now study the varying shades.

Golden-haired Suzanne is white and rosy like an English maiden; Margot is an auburn beauty and her skin is whiter still—pale and ivory-like; Jeanne's soft epidermis is amber-tinted, but the warm, pale orange hue of Carmen's frame is much more beautiful. It is not surprising if this latter darling has such perfect Italian lineaments, for Carmen was born at Marseilles, of Phenician breed, crossed with Saracen splendour.

Her body writhes in supple cadence, undulating in serpentine folds, and she balances herself lazily, first on one tiny foot and then on
the other, like an Arab girl; reminding me of a
lithe greyhound straining in the leash, so eager
is she to join in amorous sport.

All the light peignoirs of our courtesans are
thrown on the low piles of cushions which do
duty for chairs. These are the only seats,
together with capacious, wadded armchairs,
from whence it is almost a trouble to rise, once
you let yourself drop into their capacious
depths.

A bed, as broad as it is long, stands in the
middle of the room which is a delicious boudoir, arranged with Pompeian pillars, according to the period of the Directory. Our feminine detachment does not use the vast couch at
present.

The amazons are all naked, save their silk
stockings and dainty shoes with imperious high
heels. When a woman's charms still possess
the firmness of youth, and if she is tall and
slender besides, she shows to great advantage

in handsome hose and tiny fantastic footgear.
The sheen of her stockings is akin to the shim-
mering scales that terminated the bodies of
legendary sirens, and the feminine plump hinder
cheeks seem as if emerging from the frothy
crest of splashing waves. Garters are indispensable to complete this costume, or rather
lack of costume. Suspenders are horrible
inventions. What dry-skinned, angular old
maid, with long, protruding yellow teeth, and
scraggy legs, first sported *jarretelles?* Doubtless
the same jealous hag, hating her own sex,
imagined also that odious form of feminine
underwear called " combinations. "

Our brides of the night at the Montyon
temple wore garters, with large rosettes, their
vivid tints contrasting with the colours of the
stockings. Carmen's garters were bunches of
cherry ribbons, streaming down the side of her
calves hidden in grey silk. The effect was
delightful.

The sweet dames squat down at our feet, on
the carpet, near the foot of the bed. Their
skilful hands are busy and a languid look comes

into their eyes. Some of them sighed as if overburdened with rising lust.

Of course, this was all pure acting, but it was so well done, that it seemed quite natural.

All of a sudden, Carmen throws Suzanne down by simply seizing her neck and forcing her to bend like a frail shrub in the grasp of a sturdy gardener. Suzanne is stretched out on her back, sprawling on the thick carpet. As she fell, exposing her coral grotto, shaded by transparent floss-silk hair, through which every detail of her centre of love could be made out, she uttered a little shriek, and exclaimed :

" How brutal you are! You hurt me— you nasty thing! "

She kept on for a moment, murmuring : " Brute! Brute! " when, suddenly changing her tone, she whispered, cooing with pleasure : " Yes, yes! It's nice like that! Keep on! I do love you so—my Carmen! "

The incomparable brunette had seized fair Suzanne's legs, suddenly throwing the thighs of her little friend over her own sturdy shoulders. Carmen, on her knees, lowered her head, and eagerly darted forth her rosy, pointed tongue, which flashed into view but for an instant, as it was immediately buried in the coral cleft of her willing victim.

Jeanne and Margot followed the Lesbian example unblushingly displayed before their eyes, and we viewed with rapture this splendid group performing the mystical rites of the cult of " 69. "

After a few minutes of this Sapphic struggle, when all the girls were supposed to have satisfied their erotic cravings, whether active or passive, or both, the two groups mingled their ardent intertwinings, and pursuing each other laughingly, changed partners for a second. Then one female would pull another away and seize her for herself, while the deposed kissing queen flew to the mouth and breasts of her whilom conquest. Or one wench would kiss and lick with delirious ravishment the pretty rosy bottom of a girl, who with teeth and lips, would be actively worrying the yielding pussy of another.

There was no end to the varying combin-

ations of these wayward, writhing tribades.
Scarce could we gloat over one interesting
double or treble posture, when thighs, bellies,
breasts and backsides, shining out in splendid
shamelessness beneath the electric lights, seemed
to break away into shadowy corners of the room,
and before we had time to regret their disap-
pearance formed again into fresh attitudes.
Laughing faces appeared for a second, only to
be quickly hidden between quivering thighs,
and rounded supple buttocks moved up and
down, caressed by waving white arms. A
glimpse of features convulsed with the spasm
of pleasure—revulsed eyes, clenched white
teeth—and sculptural legs, encased in multi-
coloured silken hose kicked high in the air,
terminated by light satin shoes in which stif-
fened tiny toes could be seen working in cadence
with fingers clutching convulsively at empty
air.

At last, inarticulate cries, sounds of smo-
thered kisses and clappings of toiling tired
tongues gave place to bursts of laughter—long,
loud, and rather forced—as the girls spoke grate-

fully to each other, audaciously telling how much they had enjoyed their lewd mutual mouth diversions.

I am, however, exceedingly sceptical, so I went up to Carmen, and as I familiarly passed my hand over her velvet bosom, I ventured to say :

" I'm afraid your raptures were not entirely genuine ! "

My grand morsel of carnality smiled angelically without a word, but golden-haired Suzanne who had overheard my rude remark, put out her tongue with the grimace of a wilful child of the gutter, as she took the liberty to reply to my observation.

" What do *you* think ? D'ye suppose we're able to spend in front of all the jays who come here to see us duck to each other ? Ah, my boy, if you could only be in hiding about one o'clock, when we we've just had our lunch, then you'd see a sight for sore eyes ! Sick and tired of the men who've been all over us since five o'clock in the afternoon the day before, Carmen and I compare notes, and she consoles me while

I try by my kisses and caresses to make her feel the same pleasure as I am having. At that moment, men disgust us and we enjoy for ourselves. Is that right what I say, Carmen?"

" Rather!"

" With me—just now, my pet—how was it?"

I risked this query timidly. Despite my incredulous nature, I hoped, nay, fancied, that I had really stirred the depths of the dark demirep's sensual organisation. My reader has guessed that I had possessed Carmen for one brief moment.

I had intended to pass over this libidinous episode in silence, but having gone so far, I had better tell the whole truth. The sight of Carmen, hard at work chewing the clitoris of merry little Suzanne, had so excited me, that I pulled down trousers and drawers, and oblivious of the presence of my companions— doubly intoxicated by liquor and lust—I drove my stiff obedient member dog-fashion into Carmen's gaping grotto. She opened her thighs, as she felt my approach, and even deigned to assist my ingress with her left hand while she held Suzanne down with her right. What amused me was that she never even looked up to see which of the male visitors was ramming into her body, and I do not think she cared or even knew until I told her. Very few strokes sufficed to relieve me, and as my spermatic sluices opened, plentifully bedewing her womb, I had fancied with the customary vanity of the lord of the creation that there was some throbbing response and inward palpitation of pleasure.

Carmen only laughed at my eager question, and offered me her lips, where I gathered a long, delicious sucking kiss, which seemed to taste strangely. I drew out my handkerchief and wiped my moustache.

" My mouth tastes of Suzanne! " she exclaimed, with more silvery laughter. " Just look at my darling little girl and tell me if there's anything disgusting about her? "

I turned towards the mischievous blonde beauty, and felt a great desire for her, which I did not hesitate to formulate in plain terms.

We had ordered four bottles of champagne at twenty francs each, and for enjoying the spectacle of the private games of the damsels, we were charged at the rate of ten francs for each girl engaged. We now asked that they should show us some more fun.

Margot, of the mahogany tresses, borrowed a greatcoat of one of the gentlemen spectators, and in obedience to her request, I handed her my high silk hat. Equipped with these two articles and grasping a walking-stick as well, she pretended to have just entered the room. She looked very well indeed in her masculine get-up.

She walked round the room, playing the part of a gentleman strolling in the street, seeking for some gallant adventure, and throwing sheeps' eyes at the girls passing along the Boulevard. She, or he, feigned to fall in love with Suzanne at first sight, and approached her with a wink and beckoning finger, as if to say: " Come along o' me, little woman! "

Stopping suddenly, she turned towards the knot of admiring men—her little audience—

and opening her coat, showed us her nakedness.

What strange transformation had taken placed? Her bushy inverted triangle had disappeared, and in its place was a peculiar object fastened to the bottom of her smooth belly. It was projecting stiffly forward, and in fact, was nothing more than a phallus of vulcanised india-rubber, vulgarly known in English, as a " dildo, " and in French, as a *godmiché*. This formidable weapon contrasted agreeably with her big alabaster bubbies, which could be seen in their entirety, allowing us to admire the elastic firmness of their twin rotundity.

" What a nice girl ! " said Margot, trying to speak gruffly with manly tones, to Suzanne. " How old are you ? "

" Sixteen, please, sir ! " replied Suzanne, with mock-modest air and downcast eyes.

" Only sixteen ! Fancy that now ! " replied Margot, uneasily, standing first on one foot and then the other, as if excessive erection was troubling a randy rake. " Are you a virgin ? "

" Of course I am! I'm too young to go with a man! You bad, rude gentleman to ask me such a thing! I shall tell ma!" quavered Suzanne, pretending to cry.

" Don't weep, ducky. What does your mother do for a living?"

" She's a laundress, sir. "

" And your father? "

" He s a bill-sticker, if you please. "

" What's your name, my girl? "

" Suzanne! "

" Oho! She's sixteen; her name is Suzanne; she's a virgin; her father sticks bills and her mother takes in washing. Oh dear! oh dear!" Margot wriggles about as if in pain, and acts the part of a voluptuary seeking vainly to restrain his passions. Her hand seizes the comical artificial tool and moves up and down as if in the act of masturbation. These onanistic manœuvres appear to afford some slight relief, for, becoming calmer, the proprietor of the grand yard asks imploringly :

" I say, lovey, let me do it to you! "

" Do what? "

" You know ! "

" Of course I do ! "

" Well, what then ? "

" You must give me fifty louis. "

" With pleasure ! "

" Before ? "

" No—after ? "

" Not for me !   I've been tricked that way before ! "

" If you talk like that, I'm afraid you've lost your maidenhead. "

" No, indeed, sir, I haven't !   Just come along, my fine gentleman, and you'll soon see ! "

Fair-haired Suzanne leads manly Margot to the bed, and throwing herself backwards on the couch, covers her face with her two arms. Margot, with exclamations of delight, pulls her partner's legs roughly asunder and standing between them, passes her hands all over the other girl's recumbent frame, pressing her breast and tickling her clitoris. Suzanne twists about, as if overjoyed at these voluptuous touches, and also gives us her imitation —that of a coy lass reluctantly trying to push her conqueror away with one hand, while she covers her features with the other, ejaculating :

" Don't ! Don't ! "

Margot places the monstrous ruby nut of the false penis to her companion's gap, and with one thrust easily engulphs the whole length of the piercer, while Suzanne sobs out :

" You're splitting me in two ! You'll kill me !"

" Oh, it's grand ! Oh, it's fine !" bellows Margot, carrying out her impersonation to the end.

After about six thrusts, Suzanne, abandoning all pretence of pudicity, throws her legs over Margot's loins, and kissing her tenderly, sighs and gasps with unbounded delight.

Margot's copy of the final short drives and out, and subsequent trembling of the spending man's legs and thighs was a faithful transcript of real copulative gymnastics.

As the powerful machine is drawn out of her, Suzanne ejaculates :

" Was it nice ? "

" Lovely, darling ! I did spend a lot ! "

" Yes, I felt your hot jet spurting right up

to my heart. Now give me the thousand francs you promised me. Make haste, there's a dear!"

Margot passed her hand over what ought under ordinary circumstances to have been shining with moisture, but which was perfectly dry in this instance. Then she snapped her fingers defiantly.

"A thousand francs for *that!* I've given you all I had to give, you little bitch! paste for your pa and starch for your ma!"

After this naughty farce, Margot, who was decidedly the tomboy of the house, twisted a strip of newspaper into a sort of torch, and clipping it between her thighs, sticking it out behind her, like a bird's tail, defied us to light the end of it.

I tried my best, as she stalked about the room like some great ostrich, to set the paper on fire. The other men followed my example, striking innumerable matches. But our efforts were useless, as with a saucy wriggle of her grand globes swelling out proudly at the top of her powerfully-built thighs, she easily evaded the approach of the flickering vestas, glancing over her shoulder to calculate how to avoid the torch being ignited.

We were soon breathless and defeated. My friends adjourned to other rooms; one with Margot, and the other pairing off with Jeanne, who had amused herself all this time by putting her hands successively into the open fronts of our trousers.

I remained behind with Suzanne and Carmen.

They were charming, patient, complaisant girls. The brunette brimmed over with voluptuous gravity, alluring and majestuous, as she covered my entire frame, quivering voluptuously, with a multitude of slow moist kisses, and endearing movements of her cool finger-tips. Her blonde companion, helped to carry my feelings of agonised expectant pleasure to the highest summits. She was never still, as sprightly as if quicksilver ran in her veins, but tenderly clinging to me all the while, kitten-like and playful.

The science of her tickling touches was mathematically ordained when once she placed her hand on the sword of manhood. I suppose I had better confess at once how I finished the evening.

Warmly hugged by Carmen, Suzanne's hand deftly manipulated my standing spear and the bursting reservoirs beneath, until I could no longer withstand the masturbating torment. I begged her to desist, but Carmen's grasp grew closer and she stopped my supplicating mouth with her tongue.

Suzanne's inexorable fingers continued to slowly cover and uncover my sensitive gland, which was painfully tender. I felt that if Nature did not relieve me at once, I should die of suppressed longing. My delicious agony came to an end at last, as Carmen nibbled my tongue gently, and a burst of hot sperm bedewed the cool relentless digits of my tormentress.

This is the true caress of the artful minxes of Paris, as it was perpetrated upon my unresisting body with my full consent, and for which I was truly grateful.

Everything is beautifully arranged at the Rue Montyon. They do you well. I shall return there. Nay, I have often been there since that memorable evening.

CHAPTER III.

Rue de Londres.

One of the very first houses in this busy street, close to the Place de la Trinité, is a fine large building, where a narrow door is always ajar. Push it open, go boldly in, and do not start when a step gives way a little beneath your foot, causing an electric bell to ring shrilly. At this signal, a very amiable housekeeper will appear to welcome you in true ladylike fashion, for you must not forget that you are in the most well-ordained temple of voluptuousness of all Paris.

When you have entered the sacred precincts, the lady who has preceded you will turn on one side, and if you do not stop her, the traditional Parisian bawdy-house summons will echo in the discreet room garnished with heavy hangings destined to stifle sighs of loving pleasure. The words : *Toutes ces dames au Salon*! will once more be uttered—the war-cry of Venus. " All ladies in the saloon ! " Such is our unauthorized translation. It is something akin to the command : " All hands on deck ! " of the British Navy, and it really means that the denizens of the lupanar, who are at liberty at that moment, shall repair to the reception room and stand in semi-circular order to undergo the inspection of a visitor, who chooses a complaisant charmer—or as many as he likes to pay for—and adjourns with his selected living toy to a private room.

The submissive ladies of the Rue de Londres are neither older nor uglier than those of any other Parisian bagnio. They have been carefully picked among the best specimens on the market of white slaves. But if I take my reader under my besmirched wing to pilot him or her—for this volume, I hope, will also fall into feminine hands—round the gayest of cities by night, it is not to tell how in imagination the concupiscent client rushes into a public seraglio, singles out a wench and shuts himself—or herself—up with her. If that is all I had to say, this volume would be almost useless. By and by, after I have shown you the curiosity of this Rue de Londres harem, you may do as you like, but for the moment I hurry to prevent the affable under-mistress summoning her flock of naked, painted, and powdered creatures.

So I place my hand gently on this responsible person's rounded arm, enjoying its softness ; appreciating, too, its warmth which is felt through the silken dress material.

"Stop a moment, madame, I beg! Don't call your girls! Beforehand, I should like to enjoy the speciality of your place!"

She puts on an air of affected surprise. Her feminine hypocrisy is charming, but not being duped by her feigned ignorance, I bow, and continue .

"That's what I want! Otherwise I'm off!"

At this, she bursts out laughing and with the idea of "choking me off," rejoins in deprecatory tones:

" It's rather high up, you know ! "

" I'd climb the steps of the Eiffel Tower twice over to see what you can show me if you care to ! The view is well worthy of the ascension. At least, so I've heard. "

" You must remember that we charge a louis for each person. "

" In advance ? " is my mocking reply.

" Oh no ! You can settle afterwards, especially as I'm sure you'll feel inclined for one of our young ladies, when you've satisfied your caprice. "

Preceded by the alert and nimble directress, I begin to climb the stairs, finally reaching the fifth floor and a secluded chamber, where I am told to sit in the dark on a bench evidently placed there for that purpose. The room is furnished like an ordinary entrance-hall, which indeed it really is. An electric light hangs from the ceiling, sufficiently distant from me, so that I am outside the circle of bright light and can see distinctly without being seen.

I wait patiently, but a quarter of an hour goes by and nothing happens. I am about to grumble forcibly aloud, when the housekeeper places a warning finger to her lips and I hear in the corridor, the unmistakable rustle of feminine drapery.

One of the brothel-wenches appears. She is a tall brunette, well-built, and she stalks proudly along, her open dressing-gown of satin and lace sweeping behind her. I can clearly make out the whole of her lissom, undulating figure, and enjoy the sight of her robust legs, worthy of the goddess Diana. Her glorious breasts are bare, ornamented with two large, brick-red nipples, and the lower part of her big belly is almost hidden by her hairy undergrowth which reaches pretty near to her navel. Her arms are firm, and finely moulded, as I should imagine those of a female Spartan wrestler, and a slight tatoo mark on the forearm, near the albow, is a sign of vulgar gutter girlhood not a whit more out of place in this vision of seeming patrician beauty than is a squeeze of lemon over a fresh, fat oyster. The prostitute passes on her way, and turns not her head to where I am seated. A man follows her with

hesitating step as if about to tumble. Drunk
with desire, he walks like one who might be
intoxicated with strong wine. The newcomer
is tall, finely built, good-looking, and dressed
with care. His frockcoat, evidently new and
from a first-rate tailor, follows the lines of his
figure, clinging to his broad shoulders and
chest. His high hat glistens with the impec-
cable lustre of a topper bought at a good establishment, and his summer overcoat, worn
quite open, is lined and faced with brilliant,
resplendent satin.

He is doubtless a rich young " flat, " or
perchance an accomplice of the woman and
merely playing a part ? Perish the thought !
I must not think of such things, or I shall spoil
all my pleasure.

The gentleman goes past, as did his momentary mistress, without looking towards the dark
corner where I am. He does not appear to
have noticed my presence.

Another short wait, and five minutes later,
the housekeeper signs to me to follow her. I
do not have to go very far this time, and find

myself in a small and very dark nook. In front of me is a door, the upper part of which is formed of a sheet of glass. Its inner side is masked by a Japanese picture, painted on a square of silk gauze, sufficiently opaque to all intents and purposes for the occupants of the brilliantly-lighted room, and becoming perfectly transparent for me, crouching in the black darkness without. The effect is as if there was nothing at all hanging against the pane, and my inquisitive, excited gaze can easily distinguish every detail of the scene enacted inside the room.

On the bed, fully outstretched, is the gentleman I saw just a few minutes before following the half-naked empress down the passage.

Still I am not quite certain that this reclining figure is that of the swell visitor who was tall, well groomed and set up, like an officer in the army, or the fashion plate of a gentleman's magazine destined to show how masculine attire looks when fitting to perfection.

The male I see before me on the bed, reclining without a rag to cover his nudity, is a vigorous fellow with a thick black beard setting off features full of energy. He is a muscular Hercules, while the man I first saw was more like Apollo in a garment built by Poole.

But, as I remarked anon, it is better to banish all ideas of trickery and stifle growing suspicion.

The strong man's eyes are closed and he remains quite still, probably intending to concentrate within himself the immense satisfaction permeating his entire manly organisation. Now and again, a slight tremor, or muscular contraction causes his limbs to move or his chest to heave, when under the influence of a rapid purring attack on the part of his superb partner.

She too is stark naked, and I can see that she is a fine, healthy, young woman, with grand plump posteriors, but the muscles of her man are so well developed that she looks quite thin by comparison.

On her knees on the bed, she leans over, and seems to be examining the man's belly. What she is looking at is his enormous virile

organ fully exposed before her. The procrea-
tive staff stands stiffly up, arched backwards
towards her customer's navel, and the sturdy
pole emerges from a black bush of wiry hair.

As she caresses the instrument lightly, it
swells up still more, getting bigger and harder.
Swollen blue veins meander round the stout
staff and a bluish-red acorn-shaped head appears shining with moisture. The whole pillar
is throbbing gently. The wanton's fingers
play caressingly all around it, and she tickles
the big, wrinkled ball-bag beneath.

The man stirs uneasily, and then she lowers
her head and takes the great nut between her
carmine, pulpy lips, as she gradually sinks down
until the entire column is lost in her mouth.
How she packs the prodigious morsel away in
her throat is a miracle.

By the kicking of her client's delighted hairy
legs and the expression of serious animal enjoyment upon his features, it is easy to guess
at the rapturous pleasure he experiences. There
is not the slightest doubt that he must soon
reach the spending goal, when the sucking siren

lifts her shapely head, and sighs heavily. At
that juncture, she resembles a diver coming up
to the surface of the water to take a long breath
of relief. The splendid manly truncheon that
has been pressing against her tongue and palate
has gorged her to the tonsils and been nigh
choking her.

I have a full view of the wonderful weapon
covered with a coat of brilliant varnish, which
is simply the warm saliva of the whorish priestess. She clasps the towering tool in her
hand and playfully tickles it. Up and down the
shaft and round about the monster gland runs
the tip of her agile tongue, protruding stiffly
from between her lips for that purpose.

From the foregoing feeble description of a
man in full erection, a prudish reader might
think that this duet—or should I say clarionet
solo ?— was a disgusting thing for the looker-
on to view. But really it is not so. After
the first moment of instinctive recoil, suggested
by acquired instinct, nature asserts her sway,
and the vigorous well-hung Adam and his lascivious Eve did not seem in the least indecent.

Paris is civilized to an extent which accustoms us to accept all sorts of delicate adjuncts to the normal act. We look upon such caresses of tongue and lips as practices permissible to cultured citizens, as long as the conclusion is not perverted. On the contrary, we think that we render our copulation ever so much more efficacious when heightened by preliminary blandishments which only obtuse or morose minds dare to rail at as being culpable.

I am not of that latter class, neither are the gay and jolly fellows who think solely of fun and pleasure and who are standing by my side looking through the bright square of glass in the door. A few chosen broad-minded friends have accepted my guidance to play Peeping Tom. We are all proud of being members of the happy crowd of Parisians, sensual and light-hearted, without a thought of harming their fellow-creatures, dwelling in a tolerant town where all brutality is excluded and politeness and tact triumph in every act of our daily life.

One of our party is a Dutch gentleman, in

whose honour we have organized this explor-
ation into the secrets of sensuality of the gay
city. It is for his joy and enlightenment that
we are thus staring at this living picture of
passion, and we are all pleased to note that he
is much impressed. His half-open lips allow
his irregular teeth to be seen, and the overflow-
ing saliva of gloating carnal covetousness is
rippling at the corners of his mouth. This
burgher of the Boompjes smiles strangely, and
his dilated eyes are fixed on the lewd picture.

He says nothing, but breathes heavily and
looks straight before him.

The woman on the bed straightens herself
up and her rough-skinned companion slowly
opens his eyes. He glances down with satisfaction at his erect tool. The couple are speaking, but we cannot hear, although we can see
everything. What follows, however, is sufficient explanation of their talk.

The girl leaves her kneeling posture, and
takes her place on her back on the bed, in the
same position as the man before.

We have a good glimpse of her open centre

of love, even to descrying her thick, knobby clitoris, her hairy outer lips of a dark reddish brown, and the delicate pink inner lining with two thin curtains, so to speak, on either side, of more sombre rosy hue.

The noble work of procreation now takes place before our eyes—the simple, animal function which since the world has been a world prevents the human race from dying out.

The man presses the girl's two breasts in either hand, and thrusts his tongue in her mouth, I cannot see as well as I should wish, for the back of the randy chap's head and his broad shoulders, loins, and buttocks block out the view.

When he climbs on the couch, we can observe the wry face of the female, showing that the cudgel of abnormal size is pressing its length along her vagina, and the man's twin posterior cheeks are jerked up and down. They wrinkle into holes and dimples when he presses forward, relaxing into their pristine smoothness as he moves out.

He jogs on quicker and quicker. The light

of love throws her head to the left as if to escape his kisses and enjoy, without the warmth of his breath fanning her face, or his tongue rolling round hers. Perhaps she is thinking of some other man? Her upturned eyes show only their whites; her lips are contracted, almost snarling, and her set teeth gleam diabolically between them.

She throws her arms round his back and I remark the pressure of her hands—so great that her knuckles are quite white.

The man's backside is agitated by a quivering movement and I can see his round purse knocking against the lower end of the sheath gorged with his thick tool, buried to the hilt within.

All is over! The man, after a last spasmodic shudder, slowly gets off the prostrate woman, and as he slips from the bed I see his staff of love, with its wet top, still stiff.

I have a vision of the yawning temple of love and maternity, and its abundant signs of the recent libation. The hussey swings her feet quickly to the ground, and while her fellow's back is turned, opens the door behind which

we are standing with flushed faces. Our Dutch
friend starts back in fright, with a guttural
appeal to some sacred divinity—as far as I can
make out.

There is no cause for alarm. The obliging
whore has merely joined us to receive the ap-
plause and compliments of her little audience,
just as a Patti or a Sarah Bernhardt might welcome the congratulations of admirers after a
well sung *scena*, or a finely-acted last act. Her
motives are not disinterested, and each spectator
gives the unblushing wench a franc or two in
return for the pleasure she has afforded us. The
Rotterdam magnate, to our great astonishment,
generously bestows a twenty-mark piece upon
her, and probably as a kind of receipt, gives
her a hearty slap on her majestic bottom. Her
eyes are sparkling maliciously. and the grateful
girl tells him her name is Réjane, while with a
laugh, she passes her practised hand along the
left side of his trousers, near the forked part
of these indispensable garments. She fingers
the small packet she finds there, and is evidently
pleased with her discovery, for she murmurs

in the ear of her congested admirer from Holland :

" See you later, dear ! You'll stand a bottle —won't you ? "

That is agreed upon, for we are all parched with suppressed excitement. We troop below and are shown into a small drawing-room. The active housekeeper uncorks a bottle of champagne, and beautiful Réjane, with freshly-powdered face, and no doubt having performed antipodean ablutions, joins us with a valiantly defiant air, meaning to let us see that she is quite ready to enter the lists for another joust with the first comer, even should he be a middle-aged obese Dutchman on the verge of apoplexy, maddened by lust, a good dinner and subsequent champagne. Nor would she mind lookers-on, if her conqueror of the moment had no objection.

The line of asterisks out of the old novels might come in handy here, but I scorn such artifice and merely declare that what followed was not worth chronicling.

CHAPTER IV.

The Assignation Houses of the Etoile Quarter.

I like to vary my pleasures, although remaining within limits I have marked out for myself, and I do not think I shall be straying from my path if I wander away from the official bagnios of Paris, and pay a short visit to certain select assignation houses which, all said and done, are only brothels in disguise.

This is how it occurred, friend reader. I like to think you are my friend, or shall I say —my accomplice ? Glance at your watch. You will see it is about two o'clock in the afternoon. We have just finished our midday meal, and having indulged in a sybaritic repast, being fond of good living—gormandizers, to speak plainly—we are slightly congested. Strong, specially made coffee, with a glass or two of genuine old cognac, has shaken up our nerves, so much so that our inmost sensual depths are vaguely stirring. You grasp my meaning?

Visions of female loveliness rise up before our half-closed lids and the idea that we are going to see some pleasing bud of feminity brings a sweet smile to our faces. We are most agreeably agitated. Is it however reasonable to think of going to a brothel at two o'clock in the day? A decided " Yes! " is my answer, and in another chapter, I will conduct you to such a seraglio—but only to be a passive observer, not an acting member in any copulative combination.

This after-lunch ardour sets our blood boiling; and we fell marvellously fit and lusty. Our sole desire is to make use of this superabundant flow of erotic energy. But where shall we go? Listen to me. I will tell you.

We might stroll in the streets, especially round the Opera or in that neighbourhood sometimes known as the English quarter, between the Avenue de l'Opéra and the Rue Cambon, with the Rue de Rivoli as its base. Most pretty are the girls who walk about these thoroughfares seeking adventures. Such is their custom of an afternoon. They are very fascinating, well-dressed, and almost always quite young. Nevertheless, it sometimes happens that after having accosted one of these peripatetic beauties, the woman-hunter is forced to consult a doctor, because acquaintanceship has been complete—too complete. Let us throw physic to the dogs, and have nothing to do with such dangerous female canine pets—to be polite. Men are not half prudent enough. We ought never to be without a small phial containing a properly-dosed solution of corrosive sublimate. There is nothing like it for sterilizing the sensitive mucous membranes and enabling us to mock at all microbes.

I am gossiping on at random. It is evident that I have fared too well at luncheon and I wander from digression to digression like a garrulous old man of eighty.

But now I swear to you that I will stick to

my subject with a bull-dog grip and never leave it any more.

I purpose to take you with me to one of the assignation houses. They exist all over Paris and in every good quarter. My aim is to show you the best, and we therefore make a move towards the Etoile triumphal arch.

About twenty years ago the best quiet temple of this kind was in the Rue Duphot. It was run by a certain Madame Leroy who became quite notorious. Talk about this place to an old Parisian—a real Boulevard rake. You will hear him sigh at the random recollection and he will tell you what fun was to have been had at that sly retreat.

Peace to the ashes of good old mother Leroy! She is dead and her dwelling no longer exists, having been merged into a large drapery emporium. If I remember rightly, a Madame Lacroix succeeded her. She was also esteemed and respected by the voluptuaries of the gay capital as she extended her hospitality to delicious little angels and generous libertines. She emigrated to the Etoile district and opened another fashionable house for instantaneous unions, but soon followed Madame Leroy to the paradise where accommodating go-betweens reap the reward of their obligingness on earth.

The house of Madame Lacroix was in the Rue Lord Byron, where the business is now carried on by the sisters Dupré.

We can toss up whether we go to the Rue Lord Byron or the Rue Balzac—both close together. Near the Madeleine, within a stone's throw of each other, we have Rue Lavoisier, Rue Pasquier, Rue de l'Arcade and Rue des Mathurins. In each of these four streets are famous procuresses, but a representative establishment of this kind is carried on conscientiously in the Rue Balzac, where I therefore decide to conduct you.

So we enter the street, named after the celebrated French novelist, from the side giving on the noble Avenue des Champs-Elysées, and the abode of ready-made love is the fifth house on the right of this hilly little thoroughfare leading to the Avenue Friedland.

You cannot help being pleased with the aspect

of the small villa, which has a most decent appearance, but you will admire the interior much more. Madame V....., the lady presiding over this temple of matrimony while you wait, is not an ordinary person. She is well educated and the widow of a noted prefect of a provincial town. History says he was held in high favour by Napoleon III. The aristocratic relict of the Imperial functionary is sprightly, engaging, and wideawake, despite her sixty-eight summers. Quite the gentlewoman in her rich, though quiet deep black costume, with her silver locks worn in bands carefully smoothed down on the temples. Her white hair enhances the pure classic outline of her patrician profile. Our dignified go-between still retains her court manners. The voice is imperious in tone; sweetly resonant, however, with a true feminine ring. Her gestures are most impressive, and when she waves her hand towards a chair, welcoming you in queenly fashion, you feel that the Empress Eugénie must have made the same refined movements when at her zenith in the Palace of the Tuileries.

We are surrounded by charming luxury.
One cannot help admiring a magnificent ancient
cabinet, its panels covered with delicately-sculp-
tured figures and ornaments, while in every
corner are flowering plants and rare shrubs,
placed here and there with an eye to unobtru-
sive artistic effect. All the chairs are covered
with tapestry of quiet hues and the vistor's
glance is not offended by gaudy satin, velvet,
plush, or staring newly-gilt picture frames.
Such an elegant interior is a nice change from
the inevitable crimson and light blue hangings of
the padded and quilted boudoirs, reeking with
stale tobacco smoke, such as are seen in the
closely-shuttered licensed houses of ill-fame in
Paris.

We are now in the principal drawing-room,
where visitors are received, and it befits us to
assume a society attitude of easy restrained
grace, as though at the " at home " of some
truly noble lady. A discreet housekeeper has
summoned Madame who appears before us, and
begins to converse with exquisite reticence and
adorable circumlocution. Her talk is spiced

with two or three bold enquiries, yet without ever overstepping the bounds of good taste, and these few questions, which she lets drop with an innocent air, seem to be strident notes, as of a brass instrument breaking forth at rare intervals in the midst of an accompaniment of softly melodious flutes and violins.

Madame ventures to seek information concerning our tastes and the amount we wish to spend for our pleasures, as she has " articles " to suit all purses—all well-filled purses, I mean. You can disburse ten thousand francs, if you choose to demand the privilege of enjoying the sweet bodies of such front-rank courtesans as beautiful Otéro, the grandest Spanish dancer of the age ; or the racecourse pet, dear little Emilienne d'Alençon. As for the latter darling, I scarcely think Madame ought to have made so free with her name, because this notorious little siren has not long since been legitimately married to Percy Woodland, an English jockey.

According to prevailing tastes in the gayest of cities, Madame is only doing her duty when she proposes the best known *cocottes*, forgetting that all the most noted demireps are dangerously near thirty, and in many cases much older, but the idea that a lady of easy virtue has seen much service in the army of Cupid is generally an extra allurement for the common run of rakes.

If you have lots of time on your hands and more money than you know what to do with, Madame V... is perfectly able to obtain for you an interview with real high-born dames, noving in the best society.

" Don't you see, my dear monsieur," she explains, " dressmakers ' bills do run up so quickly, and if a beautiful creature wishes to hold her own and be in the front of fashion a year in advance with all the new creations in frocks and underwear, it costs one's eyes out of one's head !

" When indebted to milliners and seamstresses, or their modern successors, male experts in the art of draping the female figure, women —married, widowed, or divorced — whose reputation is untarnished, and are sometimes

still virtuous, can be approached and made
to put a price on their own dishonour. In
such a case, the amount is fantastically high. "

We thank Madame for her solicitude and
proposals. We have not come to see her with.
the whims of a millionaire running in our minds,
and the idea of being momentarily put in possession of something excessively uncommon
and beyond the reach of ordinary mortals does
not excite our vanity or our lubricity in the
least.

" I should feel happy to be the owner of
some unique picture, wonderful bit of old furniture, or any ancient curiosity, of which the
rarity might be the sole merit, but when
womankind is the object of negotiation, I am
of opinion that such pretty birds are not tempting unless young. "

" Aha ! I see what you are after ! " exclaims
Madame. " You are deliciously vicious !
Unfortunately for you, I detest having any
trouble with the prying police. I have nothing
to offer you under the age of sixteen. And in
the case of such youthful minxes, I should

only introduce you, and you could take them were you liked. I could not allow the little affair to come off under my roof. I don't understand such tastes myself, especially when having to do with men of the world such as you are. Don't you think that a woman—a real, ripe woman—having attained the age of reason and her legal majority is a thousand times more enjoyable than an unknowing, gawky schoolgirl ? "

" You don't quite understand me ! " I begin to explain. " Let me tell you— "

" It's quite unnecessary, " interrupts Madame, positively getting quite excited, " you should really rely upon my experience in such matters. "

She runs on, her agile tongue hard at work, and it would be useless to try and stop her. It is far better to let her chatter. When she has finished pleading the cause of the mellow matrons she has in waiting behind the wings, she stops, short of breath and arguments, and I seize the opportunity to make a quiet declaration in emphatic accents.

" I desire something not under sixteen, but certainly not over eighteen. "

" Why didn't you say so at first ! " rejoins our affable hostess, with an air of surprise, as if she had only just begun to understand my meaning. " It is now a quarter past two. In about twenty minutes, I expect the visit of two adorable young lassies, quite unsophisticated, knowing nothing of life—*débutantes*, in fact. I shouldn't be at all astonished if they were still virgins ! "

" No, really ? "

" Oh, I mean what I say ! "

" Then as far as my friend and myself are concerned, it's a case of good bye, Madame— nothing done ! "

" Stop a minute ! Whatever do you mean ? What a funny fellow you are to be sure ! "

" Not at all, dear Madame. We are not out on the warpath seeking for maidenheads, and if that was the game we were hunting, we shouldn't beat up brothels to find it. We're passionately fond of women and love a bit of fun with beauty adorned or unadorned, just as we find it. Nevertheless, we respect maidenly virtue, and therefore have no other course left than to thank you for your kind welcome, bow as gracefully as we can, and retire in good order from your amiable presence."

"Don't go away. I see now that you are real gentlemen and perfectly reasonable. Since you put things that way, I will be frank with you. No!—my two little fairies are not intact, I assure you. They might pass as virgins—that's certain, being so sweetly alluring and artless. To tell the truth, they have had connection several times, so if you please, banish all scruples from your consciences."

"'A standing member hath no conscience' is an old saying you may have heard before?" I dare to add.

The charming procuress condescends to smile at my fine old crusted jokelet and to pass the time shows us over her cosy nest, which is indeed a most comfortable, well-furnished dwelling. Each room is correct in style, nothing clashing to offend the taste of the most fastidious. Every little detail is carried out to perfection, and to quote but one instance—in each bedroom stands a bidet with a basin of sterling silver.

" I am obliged to flatter my richest customers—the Yankees. They adore luxurious comfort, especially in the way of toilet utensils. If they did not see here and there a bit of real gold or silver, they would think they were in some low-class house. "

" I suppose you have a host of foreign clients ? "

" I couldn't make both ends meet without ! Parisians are economical people even when their own private joys are in question, and they want Mahomet's houris and the seventh heaven besides for their miserable five louis. "

" Perhaps that's your fault. Maybe you reserve your choicest goods for these voluptuaries from far-off lands ? "

" Not at all. I treat all my friends—my clients always become my friends—in the same way. Rely on me blindly; explain your wants as freely as if I was your mother. Tell me what are the secret little lascivious longings that stir your inmost being and I'll satisfy you. You see it's the simplest thing in the world to get on with me."

" I quite grasp your meaning, Madame. But I warrant you have to listen to some funny confessions now and again?"

" I believe you, my boy!"

With effusive confidence, she began to get quite familiar and was continuing her discourse, when the front-door bell tinkled timidly and the housekeeper made her appearance.

" Mademoiselle Irma wishes to see Madame."

" Send her in," replied the mistress of the house with a little laugh. Then turning towards us, she went on. " This interesting young person is about to satisfy the propensities of a gentleman from Hanover who has taken the precaution to write and state his requirements. He'll be here at four o'clock. Mademoiselle Irma will await his coming and do her best to make him happy."

At that moment, a tall, fair, thin young woman glided into the room. She seemed rather nervous, and was not at her ease. Her regular features were sufficiently agreeable although she looked rather faded.

" Irma, my dear, have you got your part by heart ? "

" Oh yes ! But I'm awfully frightened ! "

" You great goose—you ! Recollect that there's twenty louis going into your pocket. No, really, you're too stupid. Let's see if you understand your task. Rehearse it a little in front of these gentlemen. That'll get you used to it. "

" I should never dare ! "

" I'm glad you speak like that ! It's a warning for me, " replied the obliging lady with solemn anger, throwing back her head and frowning. " You can go ! Luckily I still have time to find another female who will take your place with advantage. "

It is difficult to picture the emphasis with which these last words were uttered. As for fair-haired Irma, she made a step forward, and in humble, supplicating accents, entreated :

" Oh, Madame ! Pray don't send me away ! "

" I know all you're going to say, and it's perfectly useless," said the old procuress, interrupting her, and rattling on with great volubility. " I can imagine every word that's on the tip of your tongue and all I have to reply is— rubbish! Business is business all the world over. Here we have a generous customer such as you don't find turning up every day in the week these hard times. And I'm to kick him out; let him be off in a huff, and lose his patronage for ever, because this fastidious bit of skirt is timid? A nice thing for me!"

" No, no, you needn't get angry! I've got over all my fright already."

" In that case, prove it to me. Just let us see how you'll manage."

The washed-out mermaid smiled enigmatically with true adorable feminine malice, which lighted up her clear-cut features and made her almost beautiful for an instant. She was quite changed. Putting on an air of lofty pride, stalking haughtily across the little room, she took a seat in an armchair.

" Good!" said her employer. " What a

fuss you've been making about being in a funk!
You're doing it capitally. Now pay attention!
I'm going to be the man, but you musn't box
my ears—only make believe, if you please."

Madame went to the door and rapped at a
panel, pretending to knock.

"Come in!" slowly said the blonde beauty
in low, grave tones—she had an exquisite deep
soprano voice. "Well? What now?" she
continued. "Are you going to stick there
like a statue? Approach! Nearer—go down
on your knees! Here, in front of me!"

With a slow, deliberate and graceful movement, Irma lifted her scented skirts, not too
high, just above her calf, which, swelling proudly
high up on the leg, was far from being badly
shaped for a thin woman. She wore black silk
openwork stockings, and low, high-heeled shoes
of patent leather. Her foot was long and
pointed, with a high instep.

The old woman, enacting the masculine *rôle*,
thrust forward her withered little white hand,
without a single ring on any finger, and moulded
Irma's tempting lower limbs.

" How dare you take such a liberty without permission ? " exclaimed the golden - haired queen, as she lifted her tightly-gloved right hand and made the gesture of giving a blow with her open palm, while calling out in loud, commanding accents, " Kiss my foot ! Press harder ! Let me feel your wretched lips through the leather. That's right ! "

" Yes, my girl—that's right indeed ! " rejoined Madame. " So this is what you thought was terribly difficult ? "

" It's the face-smacking I can't get over ! I shall never dare box a man's ears. I'm sure he'll give me a good hiding if I do ! "

" Oh, you silly thing ! Haven't I told you over and over again that this is what he wants ? You don't mean to tell me you refuse to afford this chap the joy he's going to pay for ? Think of your own delight, too, when you touch the twenty louis ! How about the yellow gold ? Is it to be ' Yes ' or ' No ' ? "

" Yes ! Yes ! I'll do it ! Have no fear ! I'll slap his face till my hands ache ! "

I could not help laughing loudly and my friends followed suit.

" You're enjoying yourselves, I see, " said Madame, addressing us. " For the moment, I quite forgot you were there. Your little ducks ought to have got here by now. They've missed their tram, or else they've been buying sweets and haven't a penny left to pay for their ride. It may happen, also, that they are dawdling with their best boys. These fancy chaps are the ruin of these imprudent giddy girlies. It's a bit of a trot from where they live—the suburb of Levallois, which is full of these saucy cats. "

Not being in a hurry, I told Madame that our time was our own, and the minutes slipped by most agreeably as I became initiated into these peculiar ways of earning a living in Paris. Such revelations were interesting. My digestion was almost finished and I felt more comfortable and less congested.

" I expect you don't often have customers who want to pay for getting a smack on the nose ? "

" Oh yes, I do! You would be surprised to know how many Prussians adore this sort of thing. Englishmen, Russians and the sons of the Stars and Stripes are more often inclined the other way. "

" I should fancy it is easier for you to get women who strike than girls who consent to let themselves be knocked about ? "

" You're entirely mistaken, my dear sir ! As you have just noticed, a daughter of Eve is forced to make a great effort in order to overcome her natural instincts. The mere idea of lifting her little paw to a man fills her with abject terror. On the other hand, the notion of being perfectly passive and submitting to the male's brutality fits in with a woman's true disposition. When a girl is fond of a man, obedience follows as a matter of course. When, however, it comes to selling her caresses, money has to compensate the absence of affection. "

" Such parlour pastimes must be expensive ? "

" You want to know the tariff ? Getting tempted, eh ? You'd like to try this novel excitement—naughty boy ! "

"Not at all! Such diversion does not tickle my fancy, nor that of my friend, though we're both overjoyed to learn something new to us, especially when we have the pleasure to fall across such a refined and sincere instructress."

"Ah, you're trying to flatter and get round me, are you? Your compliments are thrown away on an old woman like myself."

"You possess, Madame—if I may be permitted the expression—the coquetry of your sweet silver tresses!"

"Quite poetical, I do declare! Don't get sentimental, young man, for I shan't stand it. I prefer to tell you at once a little story. You must know that if a gentleman gets too rough with a girl, he has to pay dearly, when his cruelty reaches high water mark. There's no great harm in bestowing a good slap-bottom on a forward female. She weeps and howls—then sets off laughing, and when she recollects that she's going to pouch twenty louis or so, there's no end to her merriment. She's certain to get the cash, for which mamma is responsible, and mamma is yours to command!"

" Don't you ever meet with some unscru-
pulous bounder who, after having had his bit
of a lark, slings his hook without paying ? "

" Never ! When I don't know the gent,
my terms are strict cash in advance ! "

" How do you mean—'those you know' ? "

" I should have said regular customers, with
whom I'm quite familiar, and I can assure you
they are all men of honour every one of them.
I count no suspicious characters in the whole
circle of my acquaintances. "

" Bravo ! You've explained the situation
most clearly. Now for your promised anecdote, if you please, Madame. "

" If you keep interrupting me, I shall never
be done. "

I promised to be as mute as a fish and she
was good enough to spin the following yarn :

" A rich gentleman, not a Frenchman, was
recommended to me. I hope I am not too
indiscreet when I tell you that he is the nephew
of the ruler of his native land. My new customer was possessed of weird manias. He
came here often, but I was forced to tell him

not to return any more. You must know that
in this very room not long since, I presented
to his notice a most charming young lady who
seemed to please him vastly. He passed an
hour with her, simply chatting in a friendly
way, and to show how grateful he felt towards
me for the introduction, he gave me twenty-
five louis. That was quite the act of a gentleman. But such disinterested generosity awak-
ened my suspicions. Even when a man is
immensely rich, if he hands over such a nice
little sum to a woman in my position, it s because
he thinks he's getting value for his money. Off
goes my gay cavalier, and what do you think
he had done? Made an appointment with the
lady to meet him at his own place, promising
her two thousand francs, if she would be nice
and kind to him, very submissive, and lend
herself with docility to his pretty little caprices.
This was unknown to me, and did me out of
my commission—what I call a breach of trust!
But that's neither here nor there! Fancy
now—two thousand francs! As likely as not,
the poor girl had never set eyes on so much

money in her life! One thing you musn't forget—he hadn't told her what these sunny games of his were in reality. She soon found out, as you'll hear.

" Punctual to the minute, in her best chemise and drawers, my ladyship—powdered and perfumed-keeps her appointment. The mysterious foreigner had taken care to get his servants out of the way, and opened the door himself. Too polite to be sincere, he conducts his princess most ceremoniously into his elegant drawing-room; sets cakes, fruit and chocolates in front of her, and forces her to drink glass after glass of iced sweet champagne. Then he begins to talk about his charming longings and what he expects her to do for him—and his money. He had no sooner divulged the true story of his peculiar desires, when his alarmed guest, thoroughly frightened, shrieks and wants to get away home. So he flourishes two nice, clean thousand-franc notes in front of her big, wondering eyes and this sight, added to the fumes of the wine mounting to her bird-like brain, puts the finishing touch to her state of intoxication ; her head having already been whirling round after the first bumper. So, without exactly knowing what she was about, she consented to everything the wretch told her.

" He leads her into another room at once, fearful lest she should change her mind. It was in the spring, and the weather was quite mild. Nevertheless, the atmosphere of this chamber was suffocatingly hot.

" At this juncture, my foreigner suddenly changes his tone and manner. He starts giving his orders like a master dominating a slave, and in harsh, imperious accents, gruffly commands the dazed, trembling woman to strip perfectly naked, and quickly too. Quivering all over with shame and fright ; incapable of resisting his magnetic influence thus suddenly manifested, she obeys without a murmur. She afterwards confessed to me that even without promise of payment, she would have been forced, in spite of herself, to submit blindly to whatever he might have ordained, so great was the appalling effect of the awful sensation of unreasoning terror that overwhelmed her entire being.

"One by one, her garments had been stripped off, without her master for the time being helping her in the least, merely pressing her to make haste. She could hardly undo her stays, her fingers faltering, and nervous shivers passing through her frame.

"Finally, drawers and chemise were withdrawn and kicked on one side by the frowning ruffian, who bade her pull off boots and stockings so that she stood mother-naked in front of him. She must have presented a pretty picture, as she has small firm breasts and as nice a pussy as one could wish to see—a dark, soft, curly bush.

"The fellow stares at her until she drops her eyes, blushes all over, and she feels her skin rippling into gooseflesh. Then he takes her by the arms and holds them high up, as lewdly audacious, he looks at her in front from top to toe, twisting her suddenly round, and evidently gloating over the view of her shoulders, loins, and shrinking, fat posteriors.

" She feels awfully degraded and miserable at being treated in this humiliating way, without a kind word, or a caress, for all the world like some lost animal.

" He walks her up and down the room, pressing and stroking the whole of her shuddering body; the touch of his rough, hard hand becoming entirely repugnant to her as he squeezes her bosom, pinches her two hinder globes, and forces her to trot quickly backwards and forwards with his fingers wrenching and tugging between her thighs—where you may guess.

" All this, although a martyrdom of humiliation in itself, was endurable to a certain extent, but when he showed her a bunch of knotted cords firmly grasped in his right hand, the scene changed.

" The scoundrel started striking her without restraint on the upper part of her arms, on her shoulders and principally scourged her bottom. The tender appeals of his sobbing victim had not the slightest affect upon him. On the contrary, all her lamentations seemed to double his fury and the more she groaned, shrieked, and yelled for help and them whined for mercy, the harder he hit her. Faster and faster rained the relentless cuts of the horrible knots as hard as little blocks of wood.

" She ran wildly all round the room, like a mad thing—knocking over chairs and trying to shield herself behind the furniture. She fancied she could hear her tormentor chuckling satanically at the inutility of her efforts, for when she screened her thighs and bottom, he attacked her back, and if she tried to guard the upper part of her mauled body, he took his revenge on her posteriors, now black and blue all over.

" Once in her insane flight, resembling the efforts of a captive sparrow, newly-caged, she got in a corner and pulled a sofa in front of her, crouching down behind it. Her ruthless executioner knelt on the cushioned seat, and bending over, struck wildly at his poor, huddled-up, cowering, nude slave thus entrapped by her own efforts.

" How long this atrocious punishment lasted

she could not tell. It seemed centuries. She was half dead and every part of her was smarting, burning, aching. Despite her pain, the nervous tension caused by the obsession of heartrending fear was worse than the physical torture, and this mental pent-up agony increased to its highest excruciating pitch when she found blood flowing from her wounds and dripping down her thighs.

" Too feeble to scream any longer, she knew her strength was leaving her, and feebly beat the air with her bruised arms, seeking support as she began to swoon. Seeing her weak state, her sinister torturer bundled her with many a push and kick into a bath-room near handy. The big enamelled bath seemed prepared for use, and he lifted his prey and threw her bodily in. She fainted away at once, and no wonder. The water was icy cold, at freezing point, and big lumps of ice were floating on the surface.

" When she came to, she found herself lying in bed. Her executioner was by her side, petting her and watching over her with the most tender care, begging her pardon and asking

her what he could do to alleviate her sufferings.
He explained that the yearning to act in this
incredible style was stronger than his will-
power and he experienced no pleasure with a
member of the weaker sex, unless he assaulted
her as he had just done.

" The spectacle of a woman without a rag to
her back writhing under his horrible ropes'-
ending, exacerbated his sensual passion, and
when she lost consciousness, which was nearly
always the case, an imperious call for copulation enslaved him.   Then carrying his victim's
frigid body, cold as that of a drowned corpse,
to his bed, he possessed her fully and re-
peatedly, while she was still as if dead.   As he
gradually felt her life-blood slowly ebbing back
warmly from the reaction of the glacial bathing
ordeal, his mad enjoyment carried him into
realms of inconceivable lustful bliss.   Calming
down, the vampire became himself again, bitterly
regretting what he had made his companion
endure, and seeking for her forgiveness.

" My poor little friend listened to him coldly,
merely saying ' yes ' or ' no ' to all his ques-

tions, and trying to be excessively polite with her maniac for fear of vexing him. She took heed, as you can conceive, to hide the rage that almost choked her at the idea that she had been cajoled into undergoing such vile treatment.

" To cut my long story short, I must inform you that she was able to depart at last. Tightly clutching her two thousand-franc notes, she reached home and dropped into bed at once, in a state of high fever, with occasional fits of delirium. A doctor is sent for, and he is astounded at the sight of the contusions on her arms. She reveals to him that all her body is the same, if not worse, but refuses to tell how she received the countless blows showing terrible traces all over her, merely saying that she had been beaten. Such an avowal was needless, and although reticent with the medical man, she told the truth to her lover, the nicest fellow in the world, as bold as a lion and brimming over with common sense. He confided the strange story of his mistress to a friend of his, and the two young fellows went boldly to the flogging brute's apartments. He tried to avoid seeing them, but the girl's adorer boldly plumped himself down in the hall, and sent his companion into the courtyard, so that the tyrant couldn't leave the premises so long as the two sturdy chaps chose to remain. There was no getting away down the kitchen stairs.

" Seeing they were resolute, my man was forced to have them ushered into his private room, where he had to listen and remain quiet as they informed him in plain terms that the little woman he had thrashed so unmercifully was very ill, her life being in danger. It was no use him denying anything, for it was plain that if she died he would be her murderer. The sick woman had been seen to enter his flat, and when she left, a doctor had examined her at once and could testify as to her condition.

" The whipping amateur tried to ride the high horse and mumbled something about ' blackmail ' and appealing for ' police protection, ' saying that he was about to send a servant round to the station for the commissary to come at once. This woman-beater was even audacious enough to put his finger on the button of an electric bell.   But he did not dare to press it.

" The lady's champions are seated unconcernedly facing him, in easy attitudes, one leg cocked over the other, affecting an air of sublime and perfect indifference.   The guilty man began to lose his composure.   What could he say to the authorities after all ?   He reflected that an enquiry might be made, fraught with all kinds of trouble for him, to say the least.

" His visitors then began a most interesting whispered colloquy, without troubling about their worried, unwilling host, who could not avoid overhearing such words as 'hospitality of France —a free country—justice for all—protection of women and children—both rich and poor amenable to the law. '   He grew more and more uneasy, finally stammering out :

" ' Don't you think, gentlemen, that the lady's bruises might be cured with a thick poultice of twenty thousand francs ?' "

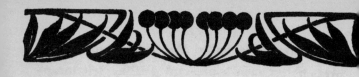

CHAPTER V.

How Venus is Worshipped in the La Villette and La Chapelle District.—A Trip from Rue Burnouf to Rue Jolivet, with Some Account of a Mystery of Montparnasse.

I had just passed a most agreeable afternoon in the hospitable dove-cote of Madame V..., Rue Balzac. My friend had told her how much he admired her talents of organisation and the countless conveniences of her snug retreat; not forgetting to compliment her on the unerring skill which she displayed in choosing delightful nymphs of all ages to gratify the sensual appetites of her select circle of customers.

He was so delighted that he refused to leave me. After such a pleasant day, he felt incapable of spending an evening at home. The night should be made worthy of the delicious interval between lunch and afternoon tea, he affirmed.

His wish to continue exploring the " double-life " resorts of Parisian Don Juans was stronger than ever. Two adorable little minxes had been thrown into our embrace. Our senses were sated—or ought to have been. While we had been with them and had pressed their plump, fresh young bodies in our arms, we had loved them madly. But the charm was broken. We had had our will of them; enjoyed them unreservedly, and we were beginning to forget them already, as no doubt the couple of cooing pigeons had already forgotten us. Our feelings contrasted strongly with those of Messalina, that Empress-harlot who was tired without ever being satisfied, while we are fatigued and yet perfectly contented.

Curiosity counts for something, you must know, and if a man's brain is fatigued by a skirmish on the battlefield of fornication, it awakens once more at the noise of new combats, and fortified by the sight of fresh lassies, calls the warrior to arms once more.

So it was settled that I should lead my indefatigable comrade down into some of the lowest depths of Parisian prostitution.

An early dinner was first enjoyed; out appetites had been sharpened by the ingenuous caresses of our brace of winsome, five o'clock beauties, and we needed fresh strength for the long night's work that formed part of my plan. Braced up anew by a bottle of old Burgundy, and having lingered sufficiently over our coffee, liqueurs and cigars, we girded up our loins and started off again.

The underground railway took us swiftly to the corner of the Boulevards de La Chapelle and Barbès, and we went down the first-named avenue, on the left side of the road, going towards La Villette.

It is a remarkable fact, although logical enough when we come to think over it, that street-walkers always like to carry on their trade in the vicinity of bawdy-houses. This occurs in every city. One brings the other, and so a market of prostitution is formed.

Saucy women without hats begin to solicit us already. Strange things come up to look at us, monstrous too and cheap—all old and ugly.

There goes one night-blooming flower of the female sex pursuing a passer-by who seems in a hurry. She positively pushes against him. This creature is hideous, thin to emaciation; with flabby cheeks; weak, rheumy eyes, and touzled grey hair. The rags she wears give out a musty smell, akin to that of a neglected, muddy mongrel. She is sixty, if a day. She comes, I can guess, from some other district, and must be tipsy, or too well-known in her own part of Paris where her former customers are tired of seeing her continually. So driven by age and hunger, she has emigrated to this Boulevard de La Chapelle.

A strolling prostitute notices the strange rival strumpet, and thus hails her :

" Hi, there, old mother Morgue ! What are you doing round here? Why don't you stick to your graft on the fortifications between the gate of Clignancourt and that of the Poissonniers?"

The hag does not answer, but clings like a leech to the pedestrian she has chosen in the throng. With bold hand, she attempts an nvestigating, lewd caress. The man thrusts her brutally from him.

" I say, old woman, d'ye think I pick my sweethearts out of the cemetery?" he exclaims with a sneer, sticking his face almost under her nose.

The witch turns away without a word, and bends her back, crushed as much by the cutting insult as by the weight of years of low submissive debauchery.

We have reached the official brothel at last. It can boast of a commanding entrance-door between two windows of a fine house with a bold stone frontage.

I would have you remark that all these second-class houses, destined for the low-priced joys of working-men, have each a *café* on the ground-floor. Anybody can go in, drink, treat the girls or not, and depart without being forced to go upstairs and perform the act of procreation—or any other act.

I order some beer, but do not touch it, nor do I allow my friend to taste the stuff, for the liquids dispensed in this lively establishment are shockingly bad.

There is a group of painted ladies in scant costumes clustering round the stove at the end of the long room, furnished with mirrors, marble-topped tables, seats and benches covered with old, stained red cotton velvet.

Two of the women come to our table and sit by our side. Stereotyped smiles wreath their carmined lips; they rub their breasts against us. Their hands glide over our knees, their fingers tickling the upper part of our thighs, as they press their legs against ours.

" Gently, ladies! Not so near, please! Don't stifle us! Let us breathe freely! The atmosphere of your boozing ken is none too pure as it is, so don't deprive us of the little fresh air there is in here! "

I do not suppose I should have been so ungallant, but really I was forced to confess inwardly that the charmers were perfectly undesirable.

They were downright ugly. It was impossible to guess their age. These doubtful beauties smelt badly. A most peculiar odour of spirits and cheap scent—where artificial musk and violent vervain seemed to be struggling for mastery—rendered their presence well-nigh unendurable.

They beg for small drops of Chartreuse. We treat them to what they ask, pay and go, leaving the cats licking their chops.

No sooner outside, having crossed the threshold of this low-down knocking-shop, when buttonholing me on the sidewalk, my friend starts a series of reproaches.

" What was the good of coming up here—in these slums? It's awful—enough to disgust me with women for the rest of my life! "

" Don't talk rot! The first really pretty girl you run up against will drive your last vision out of your mind. Besides, you're a jolly sight too particular. You ought to have led those sorceresses on to gossip and watched

their wiles with their customers. It's true that
it's a bit early, and men don't go there much
before half-past nine. We've got lots to see
elsewhere. You're displeased, I see. You're
dull and beginning to philosophise. That's a
bad sign and shows you feel inclined to drape
yourself in the mantle of your dignity and retire
early to read Schopenhauer in bed. I saw you
throw a side-glance at that empty *fiacre!* You
were within an ace of hailing it and beating a
retreat. Patience, my lad—just for a minute or
two! Christopher Columbus asked his sailors
to grant him three days' delay and he'd find
them a new world. Allow me only three
minutes' grace and I'll fish you out a new
girl!''

Here is the Rue Charbonnière, in a diagonal
line reaching to this Boulevard, with which it
runs almost parallel. Let us go through it, on
the right-hand side.

'' Do you see those doors ajar, a streak of
light gleaming through, while the heavy shut-
tters, hermetically closed, shut out the view by
day and night?''

As we pass, these portals are slowly opened. Bareheaded women beckon us to come in. We turn away. They are not prepossessing, simply common sluts, serving as waitresses in low *cafés*.

In this thoroughfare, the drinking-shops, full of girls, have two entrances. One gives on this Rue Charbonnière, and is the mysterious gate of lasciviousness for the lustful wayfarer who wants to get into the *café* without being seen; the front being on the Boulevard de La Chapelle, where we find the usual wine-shop and zinc counter.

Rapidly passing in review this repulsive troop of trollops, we cut through a little alley, and find ourselves again on the Boulevard—at the corner, where there is yet another public harem.

" It's a loss of time to go inside. The wenches are as ugly and as old as in the one we visited just now. As the night grows older, I will show you a model establishment of this kind, where studies of sexual aberrations may be made if you care to note the weaknesses of

your fellow-men when stirred by strange neurotic love-manias. Meanwhile, you cannot do
better than stroll with me along the big Boulevard. "

Beneath our tread, the earth trembles,
shaken by the thunder of a passing train. We
are on a bridge over the Northern line.

" Look at those skirted shadows gliding in
the gloom, flying from the crude light of the
gas lamps. They are the streetwalkers again,
pressing under the archways supporting the
Metropolitan railroad, which here, for a brief
distance, comes out of the ground and runs
along the middle of the broad avenue.

" Let us draw near these female outcasts.
You will see that they are not a whit more
comely than all the others we have stared at in
these parts, " I tell my friend, exhorting him
to be gentle. " Listen to what that one says
to you as she trots by your side. "

" I see what it is ! " she whines. " You
won't have me, because I'm a bit off-colour.
Tain't my fault. I'm only thirty, and I look
fifty ! I don't, you say ? You're too polite to

give me right. Just as you like, but I reckon you'd change your tune if I showed you my little sister. She's a beauty and no error! Only fifteen, and awfully fond of nice, well-dressed chaps—like you! "

She takes his arm.

" Let her be, " I whisper. " You musn't drive her away, until you've seen what her game really is. Don't be so hasty! "

The wan, worn woman calls out :

" Kid ! Come along over here! "

A tall, superb young damsel makes her appearance out of the dark arches. She is dressed as poorly as possible. All she has got on cannot be worth twenty francs. But she carries her scanty cotton blouse and cheap skirt with the innate graceful elegance of a Parisian girl. She has fine, large eyes, their velvet glances lit up with the promise of soft caresses. Quite royal is the poise of her shapely little head on her long, full, flexible neck, already almost as robust as that of a full-grown woman.

My wicked friend grasps the upper part of her arm at once—probably to feel what condition she is in—so I do not ask permission to press the biceps that is free. It is round and firm. Truly this miss in her teens is a divine piece of Nature's handiwork. Her small, pretty features are brimming over with intelligence ; her face is truly delicious. But my friend should not let himself be dazzled by the light from her wonderful eyes, full of moist languor. There is deceit in the enchantment of her divine orbs.

For the moment I admire her pulpy red lips, with their plainly defined Cupid's bow, showing up so well on the dead-white ivory pallor of her full cheeks, covered with a slight down—scattered golden threads. No—the comparison is not quite true. I should have said the bloom of a peach—a delicate, ripe hot-house peach, full of perfumed, savoury juice. She has a little love of a turn-up nose, with quivering nostrils, as if Eros himself with a masterly sculptor's thumb, had modelled and chiselled it out of Venus's own flesh.

Our darling gutter goddess is, as I have said, wretchedly dressed, but she is neat and clean.

The coarse tulle twisted round her swelling neck, and tied in a big knot under her pale pink shell of an ear is immaculate. The natural talent of a *Parisienne*, when it comes to decking herself out, is shown at once in this instance by one clever detail. She has managed to discover a necessary piece of luxury—her well-polished small kid shoes. They are cut very low, showing the extraordinary rise of the grandly-arched instep of her narrow foot.

My companion's admiring eyes are starting out of his head. He is so surprised at discovering this pearl above price in the mire that he can hardly speak.

Paris is perhaps the only town where such miracles arise. In these populous quarters of La Chapelle and La Villette, I have met fifteen-year-old maidens, marvellously beautiful, with bodies of fully-developed women. Their beauty is short-lived. Soon the crapulous and brutal exigencies of their fancy-man cause their freshness to fade. The Orient sheen dies away from the pearl. Worn out before her time, the bloom faded from her complexion, her breasts flat and soft, her genital organs stretched and flaccid; the anæmic ghost of her former self, with some garish frock and a big hat, descends to the more fashionable part of the town and seeks to sell herself for a higher price, by traipsing round the Saint-Lazare Station, the Rue de Provence, or in the Chaussée d'Antin. She does this so as to be near the Rue de la Victoire. In that street is a furnished house—where for six francs may be hired for one hour, or for all night, the price being the same, a small flat comprising sitting-room and bedroom, quite nicely furnished.

All these splendid young girls are doomed to be ruined, body and soul, by the power of the " ponce "—as the harlot's master and bully is termed in English slang. Such is the result of French laws regulating the social evil. The illogical incoherence of these decrees ; blind Police brutality ; the prejudice—sad relic of bygone barbaric ages—against these wretched waifs, all conspire to drive to the lowest pit of hell the woman who tries to get a living out of her beauty in the same manner as lords

of the creation strive to sell their intelligence.
The whore is hunted down and despised; those
who should protect the weak and the humble
turn from her, so she finds herself at the mercy
of her pitiless pimp who tries to exploit her.
He is often a policeman in plain clothes set to
watch her and becoming her accomplice in return for the money he tears from her, which
she gets from her anonymous lovers among the
general public.

While these thoughts run through my brain,
my fellow explorer has not lost his time, laughing and talking with his new-found pet. Stirred to the marrow, in true ecstasy, his glance
never leaves the face of the fairy vision. He
is conquered by the girl and now it is her turn
to seize him by the arm, dragging him away
with her. Her luminous smile, assisted by
the touch of her hand, has done the trick, and
he is off without a word of apology to me—his
patient guide.

I run after him with a last word of advice.

" Don't give her more than two francs! "
I whisper in his ear.

He shrugs his shoulders and frowns at me with annoyance. He thinks I am needlessly and stupidly bothering him—perhaps jealous of his lucky find. He forgets that I am not struck by his dream of delight, and that I am full of prudence. I forgive him, and take a mental oath to safeguard him from any harm that his inexperience may bring upon him.

A whole hour goes by before he reappears from the wretched, dirty, vile furnished hotel in the Rue Caille, where this nymph of the pavement has taken him. Following her agile footsteps, he has gone down a dark passage— long, damp, and musty-smelling—his heart full of eager joy. The expression of beatitude shining from every pore of his happy face is only to be equalled in holy, religious pictures representing one of the elect being received into Paradise and about to taste the felicity of heavenly repose among the saints.

Sixty mortal minutes do I pass alone on the Boulevard, doing sentry-go, pestered every second by these hordes of street strumpets, all repulsive, and I am watched from afar by their murderous-looking, vigilant bullies.

While cooling my heels, I witness a comic incident, as a jealous girl quarrels with her lover.

" You ponce ! You dirty pimp ! " she shrieks, threatening also to denounce him to the police. Her voice is hoarse with rage.

Her man goes towards her, but at once she flies at him, dealing a shower of blows with her umbrella, shrieking at the top of her broken voice, " Help ! Murder ! " as though it was she who was being assaulted.

The wretched male, I can see, is more troubled by her strident howling than by the thrashing he gets from her gamp, and he retreats, followed by the awful voice of his raging mistress.

" Yes, I'll go to the police ! No power on earth can stop me, and I'll tell 'em that you're a thief—pimp ! Dirty pimp ! They shall know how I keep you—how I lay down my body to everybody for you—how you send me out in the rain when I'm unwell ! Oh, you rotten ponce ! You beast ! Help ! Murder ! "

Her loud yells travel far through the still night air, above the dull roar of the traffic. Round the quarrelling pair soon gathers a large crowd, mainly composed of more be-rouged girls and ugly bullies. All grin and mutter ribald remarks. Annoyed at being thus disgraced in the eyes of this select audience, the man plucks up courage and throws himself on his bawling assailant. Despite her cries, he tears the bent umbrella from her and twice slaps her face with all his might. His stinging heavy blows cause a change at once. The shrew is tamed. She now supplicates, sobs, and begs his pardon. By means of kicking her backside with his heavy boots, her liege lord drives his prey before him towards their pitiful home—the hideous furnished hotel garret, where they sleep off their absinthe, join their carcasses in rutting union and fight like two hyenas imprisoned in the same cage.

Here comes my fellow criminal at last! He looks sheepish—happy and vexed at the same time.

" What's the matter, old man? But I

needn't ask. By the way you take my arm, and cough uneasily, I guess you're dying to tell me all about it. Confide in your faithful friend and relieve yourself. I'm all ears!"

" What a marvel of Nature!" he began to reel off at top speed. " A perfect body—and only fifteen! Never saw such a bosom! Her breasts are large, round, firm, and elastic—real saucy bubbies with stiff rosy nipples pointing to heaven like threatening spear-points. And then her arms and thighs—hard and muscular as those of female Spartan wrestlers; her skin exquisitely soft and satin-like. Her legs are long and slender, such as the Greek sculptors show us on their statues of Diana."

" The little girl has sent you right back into antiquity, I see!"

My remark makes him drop high-flown comparisons and he is off again.

" You may laugh and chaff, but she is really beautiful! Nothing can be more exciting than her perfect form—that of a young girl with almost matronly charms. She is in her teens, and although slightly built, is well covered with plump flesh. Can you realise it? Can you imagine the entrancing contrast? Words fail me! I can't describe her. There's everything a painter could wish for—colour, line—an ideal model!"

"Nevertheless it seems to me you look a bit out of sorts? Have a cigarette!"

"First of all, she asked me to make her a little present. I gave her a louis. She turned the coin over in her hand, and then asked me if it wasn't counterfeit. I had to call the wretched waiter, or boots, or whatever you call him, and send him out with it, to get change. But when he brought back twenty francs' worth of silver in one and two-franc pieces, it was he who tried to pass off some false coins. Happily, I had my eyes open, and my vigilance was rewarded by a divine smile!"

"That's all very well, but if, as I told you at first, you had given her a couple of francs, which is the tariff of La Chapelle, you would have been treated better, and with respect. The fact of waiting for change didn't trouble you. There's more behind!"

"You're quite right and I agree. I could kick myself for neglecting your advice. The little darling, having stuffed all the silver in her purse and the purse in her stocking—which, by the way, formed an ugly bump quite destroying the eurethmy—didn't want to undress. I had to beg her to do so. She only consented when I showed her a bright, new five-franc piece, taking a solemn oath that she should have it when I had seen her stark naked.

"Off went every rag at last and my ecstasy at the sight of her Eve-like plight annoyed her greatly. My pleasure at that moment was, I assure you, purely æsthetical. Of course, she couldn't understand, and I could see she despised me. What wounded my feelings most was when she refused me a kiss. Do all I could, I only succeed in getting her to turn her cheek to me, when I was thirsting for her lips. She smiled continually and I could see her splendid white, gleaming teeth, driving me mad with yearning to suck her mouth and have her tongue rolling round mine. I went so far as to offer her a hundred francs for this moist embrace. Would you believe it—she refused!"

" I do indeed believe you, and I say again that if you had opened the ball by offering forty sous, the ordinary price for a short time in these parts, you could have had fornication on the bed with the woman throwing her clothes up. If you had made your agreement beforehand, five francs at a time, you might for twenty francs all told, have been indulged with any fancy tricks you may have dreamt of."

" I plead guilty. Nevertheless, I regret not having offered a thousand francs for that kiss. All my divine enjoyment is spoilt when I think how incomplete it was without that piquant concomitant—the yielding woman's wet kiss of love and passion ! "

" You wouldn't have got it for untold gold ! She smelt a rat already, on account of your gold piece, and most likely took you for a coiner, or a forger. She grew more suspicious still when you flourished the hundred-franc banknote. But when you proffered a thousand francs, her conviction that you were a criminal became irrevocably fixed in her bird-like brain. If the man had gone and changed any notes, he would still have brought you the change in silver, or perhaps, to establish a reputation for honesty and curry favour with the police, he might have had you arrested. You could have cleared yourself easily, but in the meantime, you would have been in a very uncomfortable position."

" That's true! I shudder now—seeing the dangerous risk I was running!"

" As for the kiss she refused, that is nothing to marvel at. It is quite natural. Many pretty girls will grant a man all they possibly can, and then refuse some trifling favour—a mere side-issue. I'll prove that by a little experience of my own. One evening, I was strolling in the Rue Vivienne, near the Bourse, when I stood petrified in front of a superb brunette, with eyes like live coals. She was young—only seventeen, as she told me later—and was a workgirl, seduced, and driven on the streets by her betrayer, too lazy to work. We were soon in a hotel room. By the way, what sort of a place did you tumble into?"

" Don't talk about the horrid hole. Tiled floor and a bed. Oh, that bed ! Of course, I couldn't expect much for the price they charged —sixty centimes ! I left the fourpence change out of a franc to the waiter. "

" That's the correct charge at La Chapelle, and two sous as gratuity would have been ample. What Englishmen say is right. A real gentleman should neither be conspicious by meanness or generosity, adopting the prices of the part of the world where he finds himself. "

" But how about your story ? When you were in the room—more comfortable than the one I've just left, I suppose—what happened ? "

" Simply this : after the usual preliminary caresses, and having paid the lady in advance for her precious favours—she was very amiable and tender—I considered I had a right to plant my spear in the hired territory, but she stopped me advancing directly I attempted to make her mine—as they say in the novelettes. "

" Really now ? But what reason did she give ? "

" She made a peculiar proposition. 'No !

no! anything but that!' she exclaimed. 'You're young—you seem a lusty sort of chap, by what I hold here in my hand, and in spite of myself, I think I should feel pleasure with you!' 'I hope you will!' I replied, interrupting her. 'It's nice to enjoy with a woman, but if we feel our own pleasure reciprocated, our sensations increase tenfold.' 'What you say is lovely,' she rejoined, 'and shows that I'm right to refuse you. You're a real, strong, loving man and I'm not going to be unfaithful to my sweetheart. Why won't you let me *kiss it* for you nicely? It's delicious, and men are mad to have their pleasure in a woman's mouth. You'll see how beautifully I suck.' I refused and stuck out for natural copulation. 'No! I don't like it that way,' I kept on repeating. 'When I grow old, perhaps I may fall so low as to wish my last flicker of voluptuousness invigorated in that shameful way by the warmth of a woman's mouth and tongue, but for the moment I prefer the old-fashioned style of conjunction!' All I could do or say, in anger or in jest, was in vain. My weird charmer stuck to her guns and would not give in!''

Thus conversing, my friend and I covered some little distance. The weather was fine and the walk enjoyable. We found ourselves at last at the corner of the Rue de Kabylie, a famous hunting-ground for prowling prostitutes. Among these hungry harlots, now and again could be descried some good-looking lass, with clean petticoats, and neatly shod. Most of these nocturnal birdies when they manage to run into a trifle of money, invest in new frocks, big hats and feathers, and start in a new neighbourhood at the Place de la République, where they are allowed to sit unaccompanied outside certain *cafés*. In that manner they are on show, under the lights, exhibiting themselves to passers-by.

Between the Rue de Kabylie and the Rue de Tanger, there is another licensed brothel, but it does not deserve a visit. The one I sketched at the beginning of this chapter is identical. I told my friend I would take him to Montparnasse and let him see something similar, but more typical of bawdy-house mysteries.

For the present, I led him along the Boulevard. where we had paced on the right-hand side. We now changed to the pavement on the left.

Here was the Canal Saint Martin. It is extraordinary how the advent of electric lighting along its quays has changed the character of the quarter, formerly terribly dangerous at nightfall. The vilest footpads hid themselves among the barges, and when one of the sirens of the Boulevard had succeeded in enticing a well-dressed wayfarer to the water's edge, the thieving bully would make his appearance knife in hand. A stab is soon dealt, and the wounded victim bundled over the side of the wharf into the dark waters which, with a splash, closed like a funereal pall over the corpse of the victim, after his pockets had been rifled by the sinister siren and her accomplice, "ponce" and assassin to boot. A man must have been either very ignorant or very daring if he ventured to pass along the canal banks from the Faubourg du Temple to La Villette after nine o'clock at night. Thanks to electricity and the police-cyclists, this shocking state of things is entirely altered. Greater security reigns in that part of Paris, although there is a corresponding loss in picturesqueness.

There is a small hotel at the corner of the the quay and the Boulevard. As we draw near it, a woman comes out. She quickly perceives us and beckons, turning back towards the door of the house she has just left. She re-enters and stands at the foot of the staircase, as if certain that one or the other of us, or perhaps both, will follow.

" Oh no ! She's simply awful ! " exclaims my companion.

" Your judgment is correct, but don t despise these hags. If you're polite with them, although firmly refusing their invitations in such a decided manner as to plainly show that personally they have no chance, you may succeed in being introduced to some girlish prostitute just starting on her career. She may be as beautiful as the novice with whom you had an adventure just now. Don't you think a little diplomacy is profitable sometimes ? "

Once more we repair to the other side of the

road, along the left side of the Boulevard. We reach the Rue de Meaux, where honest toilers and the worst category of loafers rub shoulders in the same wineshops. In this street, which we were able to pass through because we had taken the precaution to dress rather shabbily, we saw some good-looking specimens of feminity, between the ages of fourteen and sixteen, making their first steps as street strumpets under the tutelage of their " ponces. " These strong-stomached gentlemen profess to adore their pupils, but do not prevent them profiting by the casual offers of generous burghers. On the contrary, when a likely amateur appears on the horizon, the pimp signals the arrival of the moneyed stranger to his little woman, and after whispering a few warning words in her ear, gets out of the way discreetly. The girl, now alone, tries to fascinate her prey with many a lascivious patting touch and enticing smile.

If the beauty of the young bud is worthy of the sacrifice of your time and cash, it is advisable to try and get her away from this district, although it is doubtful whether she will consent to emigrate, as it were, with her pigeon. At any rate, if you are brave and resolute, and have had the foresight to pop a revolver in your pocket, you may let the girl lead you where she likes. If unarmed, it is better to curb your lust. One never knows if in these forbidding dens, the bully is not hidden in the room, which thus becomes a death-trap, where your charmer is the bait. A steel blade is then swiftly thrust into you before you have time to defend your life. "

Continuing our promenade along the Boulevard, we come to one of the strangest streets in Paris—the Rue Burnouf. This narrow alley is lined by small houses on either side and to atone for the lane not being level, a staircase has been built in the middle.

When we made our way down this thoroughfare, it seemed deserted. Now it is waking up. Out of these little, poverty-stricken dwellings women come trooping. The thin cotton curtains of basement casements are drawn aside and vile faces are pressed against the dirty panes.

Windows are thrown open above and more women lean out, waving invitations with their arms which they flourish like semaphore signals, as their persuasive cries echo in the quiet air of night.

" Come along here, my dear little fair man! This way, you dark handsome fellow! You'll see what I can do—how I'll amuse you—how grand I'll make you feel!"

There are trulls on every threshold. They step into the street and bar our way.

" Don't be shy, boys! Trust in me! You'll be so happy! There's nothing to beat the pleasures of love and it won't cost you hardly anything! Who hasn't got a franc— just one franc—for a fine go right up me?"

It is quite true that the maximum fee in this street is the small sum just whispered to us, and it is also a fact, though seemingly incredible, that by haggling, the male customer can have what he wants for half that amount. A thing like a woman can be enjoyed (?) for fivepence!

Most of the members of this cheap flock are old and ugly, but among the lot are some dainty samples of precocious childhood.

" Look at that red-haired young girl, " I tell my comrade. " She is slight, albeit her bust is full and rounded. She carries herself with a saucy swagger, not ungraceful. Her head is high in the air, and she throws her breasts forward with depraved undulation, offering the twin glories of her bosom to the first-comer. Upon my word, I feel towards her as you did towards the beauty you picked up—your chicken of La Chapelle ! "

Sexual passion, love—call it what you will —steals upon our senses unawares. Can we discuss the cause of desire, or truly explain why one woman pleases us more than another ?

The fair, spare creature, still in her teens, evidently does not wear stays. Her firm bosom juts out with insolent defiance, and its pointed nipples can be seen pressing against her clean, tight, white cotton blouse, striped with mauve. If she were dressed in any other way, or if her bodice was of a different hue, I might have passed her by with indifference— who can tell ?

The little she-devil has rapidly noticed that I desire her. No doubt I look sheepish, and she can see my confusion. She sidles close to me, and rubs against me like a kitten, so I can resist no longer.

" My dear fellow, it's now your turn to wait for me ! "

I do not stop with her for one hour as did my friend with his tantalizing Jezebel. I know the manners and customs of this part of the town and get through my fragmentary pleasure at a good pace.

I am soon back again by the side of my friend. We climb the steps I alluded to just now. The street forms a curve at the top of the stone stairs, and leads to the Rue de l'Atlas, a terrible alley of most uninviting aspect, badly lighted ; bordered by waste ground, enclosed by rotting hoardings.

Still more night-walkers—prowling, crouching. They are all fearfully old. Here stands one with the profile of an elderly Indian, dreadfully masculine, surmounting a vast obese body where lumps of loose fat are deposited

irregularly. Her shoulders and arms are thin.
Notwithstanding, her chin joins her chest ; the
crumbling ruins of her bladdery breasts fall as
low as her navel ; and her loose, enormous
belly—a cascade of adipose tissue—tumbles to
meet her knees.

"Come on ! Don't be frightened, ducky !"
chirrups the elephantine monster, a piping
treble issuing from this living mass of flesh.
"I'm not hard to deal with. Ten sous will
satisfy me, dearie ! You won't ? Don't say
no ! Well then, give me five sous, and I'll do
anything you ask me ! That'll suit you, my
darling, eh ?"

"Let us take to our heels and escape from
this gruesome vision. Perhaps, however, you
might feel inclined for something rather funny,
which I may baptise a cerebral amusing diversion. We could offer five francs to the horrible
virago, if she will consent to hide us in her
room behind a curtain. When she brings a
client to her wretched hovel, we can witness
the scene, so horrible as to become almost
tragical."

My proposal did not tempt my companion, and between ourselves, I was glad he did not accept it. So we turned on our heels, my friend asking to conclude our night's work at the typical bawdy-house I had promised he should see. It is at Montparnasse ; a long way off from where we were.

We jump into a *fiacre*, and I give the address —corner of the Boulevard Edgar Quinet and the Rue de la Gaîté.

The driver grumbles, but the promise of a two-franc gratuity brings a grin to his absinthiated features and his melancholy night-horse breaks into a spasmodic trot under an avalanche of lashes.

Montparnasse, like Montmartre, is a centre of prostitution. Foreigners know nothing about this part of Paris, while as for the Parisian inhabiting the right bank of the Seine, it would be more easy to coax him to New York than to persuade him to venture into this distant neighbourhood.

Rue Vercingétorix, Rue d'Alésia, and the adjacent populous arteries, are full of furnished hotels, easy of access. They are inhabited by harlots and their fancy men.

In front of the Montparnasse railway station and all round it, as well as up and down the Rue d'Odessa, these submissive sluts of the streets ply their shameful trade. In this district, the Rue du Viaduc is a curious thoroughfare, with its houses all awry on one side, and on the other, the high slope of the railway line, where the roar of passing trains is heard all day and night. The narrow, badly-paved roadway runs between. In this dark, dirty alley, couples join in the most cynical *al fresco* union, directly after dusk.

The busy Rue de la Gaîté is frequented by a mob of pleasure-seekers, less noisy and more thrifty than the roysterers of Montmartre, but one finds there the same *cafés* with song and music, and wineshops full of trulls. There are besides, several lively public balls, such as are now only known in outlying quarters like those of La Villette and Belleville, but the Montparnasse dancing-halls are fitted up luxuriously and brilliantly lighted by electricity.

I pass on quickly. To enter these temples of Terpsichore alone or with a single comrade would be an act of sheer folly. A strong band of friends ought to be formed, all fully armed; ready for any rough and tumble work, as the evening's fun often winds up with a free fight. The battle never takes place in the ball-room itself. On leaving, a side-street suddenly vomits forth a detachment of young thieves and "ponces," one of whom has probably "spotted" the stranger during the night, and thinks there is a likelihood of his purse being well-lined. If you flourish a six-shooter, the murderous lads drop back at once, but if they find you unarmed, you may rely upon being butted, robbed, and knifed; or knocked senseless into the gutter by blows from a knucklebone of mutton.

So we pass into the usual drinking-saloon on the ground-floor, fitted up in poor, shabby style, and badly lighted, as if the management was inclined to be niggardly. Nevertheless, the room is almost too well illuminated, as the women are so horribly hideous, that I rather think greater darkness still would have been an improvement. They are so thin, too, evidently badly fed, and their gaudy, shoddy silk dressing-gowns and cotton-backed satin boots are stained, faded, and frayed.

My sweet acquaintance has perceived my arrival and comes towards me laughing with all the added attraction of her big white teeth and enormous black, blubbery lips, for Selika is a fat and sturdy negress, between thirty and thirty-five years of age.

" Will you stand a glass of beer ?" she asks.

" Can't refuse you anything, you know ! "

" All right ! But you're here too early. My eccentric friend isn't due for another half-hour. "

" Never mind ! We're in no hurry ! "

We gaze round. I am protected by Selika, who has taken possession of me, but my companion will inevitably be pestered by the other girls. As I have more experience, I tell Selika to go and sit with him, so that I become the target. One ghastly siren does not fail to attack me.

" Drinking all alone, monsieur ? "

" When I'm thirsty, I hate company. "

" Offer me something ! "

" I offer you to leave me in peace ! "

" Oh, you're not very polite ! "

Off she goes, but another takes her place, hoping that her endearing glances and lavish display of a bony neck and two vague breasts may have more effect.

" What are you going to treat me to ? "

" To whatever you choose to pay for ! "

This knocks birdie off her perch and she cannot find a reply. In this way, the six or eight half-nude females forming the staff of the seraglio come and offer themselves in their turn. When the procession has passed, we are left alone.

Customers drop in and sit down. One of the poor creatures always glides to their side, and she never fails to throw one leg over the man's thigh. Hands wander under the tables. Husky laughter and forced giggling burst out occasionally. Time-worn, silly, obscene jokes are made. The Lovelaces of this parish are

not very fastidious in their amours or they
would not be here. Their chosen ladies have
no right to be very particular either—they are
too repulsive.

Selika's half-hour has gone by after all, and
the black woman spoke truly. At ten to the
minute, her client entered with faltering steps,
impelled by some strange, unknown power.
He advanced slowly and gingerly, as if there
were obstacles in his path. He held his head
down, and seemed abashed, showing that he
regretted his visit, but was too weak-minded
to stop away.

He glanced hurriedly towards the negress,
looking out of the corners of his eyes like a
silly, frightened schoolboy. The black, massive fairy drew herself up victoriously. Her
bearing was arrogant. A smile of conquest
illuminated her dusky features. Just a minute
before, she had shown herself with us as a
jovial, laughing, good-natured trollop; great
guffaws shaking her opulent bust and her swelling, pointed belly. Natural gaiety oozed out
of every pore of her voluminous, buxom body,

and merriment with malice shone in her great
eyes, starting from their sockets.

At this juncture, she made violent afforts to
enact the part of an overbearing, domineering
empress, and although our talk had nothing to
do with these sentiments of suzerainty, she
called out as loudly as she could in a gruff
voice, energetically emphasising her exclamation
with a jerk of her gorilla-like paw :

" I make slaves of all men ! "

Her poor old customer started and then
trembled. He looked at Selika with a submissive air, imploringly. His appealing glance
would have softened the heart of the devil in
hell. The black queen was pitiless. With
features hard set and mouth closed, she frowned,
staring at him fixedly with a threatening
expression. He was forced to drop his eyes.

I now looked at him more attentively, sus-
pecting some secret drama of lechery. I tried
to divine who he was ; what his social rank
might be. He was soberly and neatly dressed ;
scrupulously clean, and had evidently taken
some pains with his toilet. I put him down

as a prosperous tradesman ; perchance a notary, solicitor, or in some other law business.

Meanwhile Selika had risen, and strutted towards the old fellow, her nose cocked as disdainfully high as such a flat proboscis could reach. She threw her big breasts forward, turkey-like, trying to stalk along majestically, but she failed ignominiously. The turkey had now changed into a big, black hen picking her way in the dirt of a poultry-yard.

Her man shivered all over convulsively. Selika stood boldly, exultantly erect in front of him, staring him out of countenance, looking him up and down.

" So there you are again, eh ? " she said scornfully.

He was in a state of suppressed emotion, and could only nod affirmatively. No doubt his throat was so dry and choking that it would have been impossible for him to have uttered a syllable. Selika thrust her hand towards him, with a right royal flourish. He seized her swollen, jet-black fingers, and bending over, pressed his lips to her knuckles. The most perfectly-trained courtier of the Palace of Versailles could not have kissed the diminutive digits of Marie Antoinette with more humble, graceful gratitude.

Selika drew back, and swinging her overgrown arm, her enormous stout hand spread out, slapped his weazened, shaven face with all her might. The noise of the stinging blow resounded through the dirty *café*.

The smitten man rose from his seat and fell on his knees, stumbling forward on to his hands. Thus on all-fours, he kissed the great patent leather shoe that compressed the enormous mastodont foot of the dusky dame.

Then only did she deign to sit beside him.

None of the other persons in this bawdy-house drinking-bar had stirred. The waiter near a little counter, stood half asleep, waiting to take any orders. The female cashier, enthroned behind lumps of loaf-sugar, arranged in little pyramids, and odd bottles full of red, green, and yellow transparent spirits, looked up with a faint smile which she suppressed at once, governing herself by a feeling of professional etiquette. The painted harlots were quite indifferent, and even the only two clients present besides my friend, the old man, and I, seemed to have noticed nothing extraordinary through the thick haze of tobacco smoke.

The wretched old man sat down again. His shoulders in his ears, all his limbs closely drawn together, he made himself as dwarf-like as he could, behind a table where his bronze Venus had imperiously motioned him to sit. She ordered a bottle of champagne.

Throwing one of her giant legs over the thin thigh of her elderly swain, she placed her right hand on the table and worked her fingers to and fro in front of his eyes. He turned very pale and closed his eyelids.

The great inky hand disappeared beneath the marble slab of the table and evidently did not remain inactive, judging by the movement of the woman's arm.

Twisting uneasily about and groaning, he looked at her with poor, weak, supplicating eyes. He tried to push Selika from him, in a nerveless, childish way, exerting no apparent strength. Quietly frowning, and smiling cruelly, she continued what was certainly some agonising, gripping game of masturbation. She held this debauchee as a captive by the inhuman touch of her tugging fingers, and the tearing of her pointed, violet nails. Her onanistic mixture of pain and pleasure laid him low beneath her yoke. He was her slave, incapable of resistance. The fearful sable claws tore his flesh and scratched their way into his brain at one and the same time.

She went on with her torture, one hand concealed in the folds of her petticoat spread out over her victim's knees under the table; her left hand holding her glass of champagne.

" No ! No ! I beg you—leave me ! " gasped the moaning wretch, beads of perspiration starting on his brow.

She looked at him fixedly, her great eyes dilated, as she said deliberately and solemnly :

" Such is my desire ! "

" Yes, yes ! " groaned the old man. " If you want it—if you command it—then do it ! Anything for you—anything—everything, my empress, my beautiful mistress ! "

Her arm moved violently—the man stared at her like a bird fascinated by a serpent. Then his pupils were upturned until only the whites could be seen. His features were twisted with pain, and a slight, white froth bubbled at the corners of his thin, pale lips.

Selika's right hand appeared on the table again. She drew forth a handkerchief and wiped her fingers. Then there was a crimson streak on the white cambric, but she rolled it up hurriedly and hid it quickly.

She was the laughing, light-hearted nigger girl again, chattering and joking.

The old man, his eyelids red and weeping, his poor wrinkled face drawn and yellow, threw a hundred-franc note on the table. He rose with difficulty, pulled his overcoat tightly about him and fled precipitately.

Selika triumphantly flourished the precious little square of paper over her head.

"Isn't it funny ?" she exclaimed, coming to-wards us. " Every Friday night at ten to the minute, I act the same little scene !"

CHAPTER VI.

The Brothel of La Farcie;
No. 4, Rue Joubert.

I am now in the best managed lupanar of the Gay City; and one of the most respectable—if I may venture to say so. It is also the oldest established mansion of the kind; therefore it would be a pity if it was allowed to drop down. For the sake of old memories, I hope it may flourish for many a long day—as many days as it counts nights. And what nights, my merry men! During the rollicking times of the Second Empire, it was at La Farcie's temple of erotic delight that the most illustrious men about town—the jolly fellows who held high revel in the well-nigh forgotten "Grand Seize" private saloon of the Café Anglais—revealed to their mistresses, and to their wives also, sometimes, the mysteries of Sapphic worship.

In those days of debauchery—we have grown quite virtuous under the rule of the Republic, it appears—there was less talk of hygiene and open-air sports. Don Juans were wine-drinkers and fast livers. A fashionable fop was adored by high-bred dames from the Court of the Tuileries, but that did not prevent him being a good customer to real courtesans whose calculated caresses gave him fresh life when released from the arms of his aristocratic mistresses.

No. 4, Rue Joubert has always been able to boast of a first-class circle of amateurs, composed of men of rank and standing, the bright stars of literature, art, the law-courts, commerce and finance.

Not long ago, a celebrated politician died suddenly in one of the luxurious bedrooms. During the enquiry made after his death, it was elicited that this member of the Chambre des Députés was in the habit of coming here on certain fixed days and shutting himself up

with two of the fascinating boarders. What
the loving trio used to do will always remain as
great a mystery as the true story of the legis-
lator's tragical end.

Another little anecdote of this historical
harem tells of an adventure when a father of a
family, full of juvenile ardour, happening to
slip out of one of the cosy bedchambers, was
unlucky enough to stumble up against a youth
who turned out to be his eldest son.

" Wretched boy ! " quoth paterfamilias.
" You—in a brothel ? What are you doing
here ? "

" Don't get excited, pa ! I've only come to
claim the umbrella you left behind yesterday ! "

Many other tales could be told about La Farcie and her clients. But why " La Farcie ? " Why
that curious name ? Most people generally believe it is a real one and innocently write or
speak of " Madame La Farcy. " That is
wrong. This appellation is a *sobriquet* jokingly
bestowed upon the first matron who started
this establishment, because she was *farcie* (*i. e.*
stuffed), with malice and cunning. This must

have been years and years ago, for the brothel is as old as the street it is in.

Since this bawdy-house was first built, it has often been re-decorated, but always in a rich, quiet manner. There is nothing vulgar or glaring in its scheme of colour. All the furniture and hangings are of sober hue; slightly old-fashioned, thus wonderfully enhancing the carnation of flesh-tints and the violent notes struck by the bright shades of the sultanas' frippery and flowers.

The housekeeper introduces me discreetly and gently into the principal reception room— mirrored from floor to ceiling. She utters the traditional summons, *Ces dames au salon !*— " Ladies ! to the drawing-room ! "

In reply, the room is filled at once with a busy, rustling, chattering swarm of half-naked women. Then they are silent and stand elbow to elbow in a long line. Each beauty throws open her dressing-gown of garish brocade, showing without stint, pink marble flesh, or amber skin of warm tint, on which a tuft of black moss catches the eye. Whether brunette,

blonde, or auburn, the entrancing wench seeks
not to hide the curly undergrowth shading her
cleft, while with both hands they hold out
their rounded breasts—snowy mountains sur-
mounted by tempting strawberries. Their eyes
glisten with merriment, and audacious lewd promise. Their reddened lips are parted to show
the double row of milky teeth, whence issues,
serpent-like, the point of a crimson dart, flut-
tering to and fro, popping in and out, signal-
ling that they all know now to use their tongues.
At this moment, I appreciate to the full the
sober taste of the entire upholstery plan, for a
scarlet woman in her war-paint would be much
less beautiful against a staring background.

My desire is slowly brought into action,
fostered by indecision, hesitation, and the wish
to coolly choose a worthy partner. There are
so many different styles of womanly perfection
before me that it is almost painful to have to
make a selection. This ordeal, when my brain
is obscured by the vapours of slowly-welling
lust, adds to the piquancy of my pleasure, and
does not displease me. All sensual delight, to

be complete, is mixed with a dash of suffering. And it is impolite to keep the ladies waiting so long for my verdict—this judgment of Paris.

The girls at the shuttered house of La Farcie are mostly young, well-built, and with agreeable features. They are splendidly trained, up to every move on the board of bawdiness.

There is a splendid piece of libidinous poetry, attributed to a lawyer, Louis Protat, and published under the rose at Brussels, in the sixties, entitled " L'Examen de Flora. " It depicts the manœuvres which every expert whore is supposed to know. The author describes the scene of a novice's reception at a brothel of the Rue Richelieu, long since disappeared, but he ought to have pictured the *viva voce* examination of a prentice prostitute as taking place at La Farcie's hospitable abode of love, where the lady inmates are taught every possible lascivious artifice. The author of this luscious poem—a masterpiece of its kind—parodied the axiom of Brillat Savarin, " a man may become a cook, but he must be born a master of the roasting-jack. " This *poeta nascitur, non fit* paraphrase was travestied by Protat, who declares that a woman may learn how to best get through the gymnastics of the ordinary act of plain—but not unvarnished—sexual conjunction, while few possess the gift of being as handy, as they should be randy. The real text of "Flora's Examination" is too free for my modest pen to retrace, but being so well informed on these knotty points, the poet ought to have known that the pleasant onanistic love-trick he so delicately refers to, is made a subject of deep and special study among the refined recruits of La Farcie's bawdy battalion.

I must once more lay stress on the fact that at No. 4, Rue Joubert, the visitors are serious, well-to-do citizens, generally legitimately married to most genteel spouses. In spite of the guarantee of La Farcie's vigilance and careful choice, denoting the absence of all danger to health, these careful, solid burghers refuse to allow their mucous membranes to touch any other delicate, moist surface of the same kind. The sight of a pink, healthy mouth—the lower orifice; or that of the cushions to lay kisses upon, slightly parted in the effort of a meretricious smile, to give a glimpse of healthy gums and a full set of real white teeth, does not tempt them. It is in vain they are offered the little protecting sheath that we call a " French letter," which our sprightly neighbours across the Channel allude to as an " English hood," (capote anglaise) supposed to be a talisman against all contaminating evil that might arise during copulation. Refined labial caresses or simple fornication are not sought after our high-class debauchees prefer the touch of a manicured hand, with its soft and warm palm, followed by the expert, tantalising, tickling play of lithe, tapering fingers. For this exercise, a female must be truly gifted. She should be as agile as a fine piano-player. Nay, more so, for in the gamut of voluptuous masturbation there exist an infinity of exercises and scales which can be much more gently graduated than on a hard ivory keyboard connected with metallic strings, or by twanging highly-strung catgut.

When a man's sign of virility is voluptuously

and tenderly caressed by the velvet hand of the
desired woman, whose hidden charms and regular features seem to reach our æsthetic
ideal; whose well-timed lascivious efforts skilfully cause our senses to vibrate—in such a
moment are not the nerves of our masculine
organisation more sensitive than the strings of
a Stradivarius beneath the play of the bow, even
if handled by a Paganini?

It is, however, perfectly certain that these
complaisant angels, ever ready to submit to
their customer's caprice, do not carry their ex-
periment so far as the final crisis—shall I say:
catastrophe? — unless specially requested.
When a rake finds himself lazy, slightly overwrought; when he is stirred by a slight lustful
obsession, appealing to the mind sooner than
to the body, there comes a momentary loss of
self-confidence. As the lord of the creation
generally expresses it, " he does not feel up to
the mark, " and these fairy-like tickling touches;
the continued contact of cool digits penetrating to the inmost recesses of his frame,
form a most efficacious pick-me-up; a tonic ap-

petizer; a needful prelude before attacking the real, centre dish at love's feast.

This is the best *hors d'œuvre* on Cupid's *menu*. Without it, the finest viands meet with but scanty welcome, being too hurriedly served; lacking proper anticipatory preparation. The mechanism of our wretched anatomy is constructed in such a way that to obtain the highest amount of joy within the reach of us poor mortals, we are forced to advance step by step, as slowly as possible.

This solid fact is known and studied in the secret nunnery of the Rue Joubert, seemingly handed down from one successive landlady to another. Each new amazon electing to reside in these barracks of the army of Venus is always interrogated on this point—I use the word advisedly—and her hands are closely examined. Her rosy palms must be soft; her fingers shapely and pretty; her nails well-kept. If, added to these advantages, she shows herself able to grasp the meaning of such useful manual exercises, she is enrolled at once under La Farcie's flag.

At the colleges of ancient Athens, where the art of love was taught ; in the tea-houses of Tokio ; in the tiny rooms of the Yoshiwara, no greater attention is paid to every detail of sensual service by which the client profits.

For these reasons, the precious mansion of La Farcie, No. 4, Rue Joubert, still flourishes and will not disappear within our time.

So much the better, as this beautiful brothel is one of the glories of France. I know an inhabitant of Melbourne, who, on being told of its renown, worked hard for ten years, putting by every halfpenny, to be able to come and spend his savings during a month's sojourn in Paris. He drove from the station to this paradise, and for about five weeks scarcely ever moved from the arms of the houris at this house.

CHAPTER VII.

Round About
the Bibliothèque Nationale
and the Bourse.

How can we account for the presence of so many woman of the town clustering in such close proximity to the temples of Science and that of Mammon?

Everybody knows that too much nerve tension reacts on our secret sensual sources, quickening our erotic appetite. This is so well known that when a tragical crime has been perpetrated, or a murder committed under particularly horrible circumstances, French detectives never fail to set a watch upon houses of ill-fame. In many instances, the bloodhounds of the law run their quarry to earth; the assassin rendering himself conspicuous by an extravagant outlay and eccentric orgies in these haunts, often distributing stolen property and jewellery to the obliging girls. (1)

(1) Thus was Pranzini caught at Marseilles, after a visit to the stews of that town, Rue Ventomagy. He had fled Paris, after doing Marie Regnault to death in 1887. He gave his momentary mistress some trinkets —part of his booty. The woman he had killed and robbed was a thorough-going demirep, possessing diamonds and money. Pranzini was a Levantine, a cross-breed with Arab blood in his veins. He was gifted in a peculiar way, possessing a virile member of exceptional size and vigour. For this reason, he was much sought after by the ladies of the *demi-monde*, who whispered to each other about his secret talents. Thus he soon had a fine connection and lived well in idleness, these never satisfied darlings paying liberally in return for his efforts in their well-ploughed fields. He was adored by Léonide Leblanc, a famous actress-courtesan of the Second Empire, full of vice and lewdness, then in her decline. She was subsidised by a wealthy member of the Orléans family who died soon after his mistress. Marie Regnault was a Lesbian adept, too, but she preferred men. She was a Sapphic succube to lovely Léonide, and enticed Pranzini away from the Leblanc creature who only heard of his infidelity to her, when the story of his crime was the talk of the town. Poor Madame Leblanc never fully recovered the shock, and died shortly afterwards. She lost a submissive lady friend—her feminine toy— and a sturdy lover. One was foully murdered and the other guillotined. Marie Regnault's throat was cut in the middle of the night while sleeping by Pranzini's side, and an emerald and diamond pendant she was wearing was bathed in blood. Her property and precious stones were afterwards sold by public auction. This costly piece of jewellery, recovered from the murderer, was bought under the hammer by a Parisian dealer in such costly gewgaws, and I afterwards saw it among a magnificent stock in the windows of his shop, Rue de la Paix, where it

This neurotic strain may be caused by the exacerbation of feeling consequent upon the committal of a crime; the thought of danger and detection which must necessarily haunt the brain of a man who has declared war on society, or simply the result of efforts of concentration in study and head-work. Again, there is a terrible upheaval of the nerve-centres brought about by the poignant anxiety of a gambler, intent upon trying to win and insuring against loss in the vortex of hazardous and problematical events. In each of these cases, the outcome is the same. The jarring nerves are only soothed by the counter-irritation of the orgasm.

was exposed for sale. Its true history, of course, was unknown to the general public.

By a strange chain of events, I met with this ill-fated ornament again. It had been bought as a wedding-present, and given to one of the most pure and angelic young damsels of the aristocracy of the Faubourg Saint-Germain. When the *trousseau*, gifts from relatives, etc., were exhibited at the time of the marriage, I recognised the fine square emerald, with its grand circle of old-cut Indian brilliants of the finest water.

I held my tongue, but I could not help thinking what the chaste virgin bride's horror and disgust would have been had she know that rising and falling gently between her sweet young breasts as she breathed, was the murdered whore's gawd, scarcely cleansed from the blood that had bathed it.

Can this be the real cause of the moving stream of wandering whores who walk round the Bourse during business hours? Is this why well-dressed, painted and powdered prostitutes sit all day outside the *cafés* near the Parisian Stock Exchange?

By dint of habit, these easily accessible hussies have acquired an extraordinary gift of hunting on scent, enabling them to single out in the crowd of passers-by the bull or bear who has won or lost. What is still stranger, is that these strolling courtesans try to cajole and allure those who are losers, and lead the worried speculator, tired and sad though he may be, to the furnished hotel hard by.

"O wonderful and sublime mystery of a woman's heart!" I hear someone exclaim. "O tender heart full of maternal compassion for those who are unfortunate; always ready to open itself to the weak and the conquered in life's battle, so that the wounded may find among the treasures of womanly pity all the consolation they need!"

In so saying, a great mistake is made. If

losers are angled for by these smiling ladies, it is because they know that the gambler who has just succeeded in making a good haul, aims much higher; while the former, driven by circumstances to exercise a little momentary thrift, is ready to enjoy any passing erotic intrigue, as long as it is cheap.

The whole of the Rue Vivienne and the Palais Royal is filled by street-walkers who flaunt themselves with slyly-lifted petticoats every afternoon in this populous part of Paris, offering their charms to the business men of the Bourse.

My starting-point is the Bibliothèque Nationale—the National Library—bordered at one end by a narrow street, Rue Colbert, where No. 8 is a curious old brothel, well-known to bookworms and literary students. It is an ancient house and is sometimes called *les Arcades Colbert*. Probably at some time or the other there might have been an archway or covered walk in this part, before the Library overshadowing it now was built.

A learned diver into dusty volumes carries his

daydreams about with him. He lives in a visionary world of his own, where he is continually intoxicated by his intellectual opiates. Let him copulate in a stable with a farm-servant tending cows and pigs, and he will evoke the paradise of Mahomet with its houris; the grotto of Calypso and its nymphs; the splendour of Bagdad and the mistresses of Haroun-al-Raschid; or the gardens of Armida and its entrancing sorceress. Any women who may be in the *savant's* arms are simple anonymous instruments of pleasure, helping him to pursue and terminate his dream, rendering it a reality, without causing him to lose a single illusion. At most, when all is over, and he has glutted his sensual appetite, may he throw a wild glance about him, realising for a second the hideousness of his sordid surroundings. He then goes on his way disgusted, weighed down by regret and remorse.

If the bawdy-house of the rue Colbert is visited at night, its amiable denizens have a most desirable aspect. It is true they have long since rubbed off their venal bodies the youthful bloom I found on the fleshy frames of the young beginners in the Rue Balzac. But despite these drawbacks, pearl powder and rouge, well-dressed hair, silk stockings, coloured satin high-heeled boots, black lace chemises, gorgeous loose wrappers, and perfumes and flowers under the glare of electricity, form a glittering combination of artificial beauty ; an environment causing loss of presence of mind and discernment, and making a man fancy himself in some enchanted castle.

A daylight invasion of a brothel is a curious source of interesting observations, but the bold seeker after knowledge must be a hardened man of the world. If this afternoon investigation tempts you, it must not be undertaken in the Rue Colbert stew. The neighbourhood of the Bibliothèque Nationale causes the bedrooms of this bagnio to be continually peopled at all hours ; the female lodgers are consequently under arms from dawn till dusk, in order to receive the successive assaults of a never-ending procession of more or less lusty males.

So, in my mind's eye, reader friend, I'll choose some other brothel.

I note in all the same grey semi-darkness, be
the weather sunny or dull.   The light in every
room is tempered to sadness, shaded by heavy
window curtains or panes of ground and stained
glass.   The gloom of the reception—or de-
ception—saloons is funereal.   Submissive sluts,
startled from their afternoon lounging laziness,
scurry down from the wretched attics (1) in
untidy old dressing-gowns.   Their hair is all
touzled—a head-dresser pays a daily visit about
seven o'clock in the evening—and their naked feet
are thrust into worn-out dirty slippers.   The
vestals' beauty is slightly faded and their pen-
dulous breasts seem flabbier than ever.

One look round and I am glad to escape.
To remain would not profit me in the least.
At the bottom of their hearts, these cloistered
charmers are enraged at being unduly troubled.
Their pent-up scorn and rage is expressed in
one bitter outburst, when they scornfully ejac-

---

(1) The private sleeping accommodation is deplorable.   The bedrooms
are mere garrets, which the commonest maids-of-all-work would find inade-
quate.   Brothel girls generally sleep two by two, for lack of room, and this
promiscuity leads to appalling sexless excesses.

ulate, *Flanelle!* (1) This insult is hurled at me
when I depart without indulging in any parlour
games of lubricity.

The truth is they were busy exchanging soft
confidences. I had called at a wrong hour—two
o'clock in the afternoon. The girls, who do
not go to bed much before three in the morning—supper is served at two—and sometimes
have to sleep all night with a customer, rise
between eleven and twelve. They then have
their midday meal and retire to their own rooms
for their nap—a siesta they generally enjoy two by
two. Thus are formed those violent Sapphic
friendships I have already alluled to. Each
public woman has her own particular friend.
Couples carry on long, merry conversations,
generally sentimental ; most always finishing by
reciprocal tenderness and compliments, with an

(1) *Faire flanelle*, or to be a *flanelle*, is French slang. One "does the
flannel act, " and so becomes a *flanelle*. This expression, the origin of
which I am unable to trace, is applied to clients who chat, drink, and
play with prostitutes, but go no further, and do not seek to have connection. Such shilly-shallying folks are in fact closely allied to customers
who come into a shop, turn over the goods, ask questions, and go away
without buying anything. What " flannel " has to do with this proceed-
ing, I know not. Perhaps it indicates the state of the visitor's member,
as limp as strip of flannel, thus preventing him from copulating ?

exchange of secrets in quite a school-girl style.

Clinging together on the same narrow couch, whispering in each other's ears, they soon find themselves with their arms closely intertwining; their lips joined in long, sweet kisses. This is the dawn of real affection; joy and happiness mingled, pleasure received and bestowed with a yearning for abnegation and the most maternal sacrifice. Such is true Lesbian love, creeping into the soul of these unfortunates whose sad trade, with its numerous trials and abuses, leads many of them to be horrified at the approach of a man.

Starting from the copulating convent of the Rue Colbert, I cross the road, and passing through the verdant Square Louvois opposite, come to the Rue Chabanais, which is also close to the Bibliothèque Nationale.

No. 12, Rue Chabanais, is a model bagnio, famous in the annals of Parisian gallantry. It may be classed as one of the best brothels of the City of Light—if not *the* best—ranking with No. 14, Rue Monthyon, and No. 4, Rue Joubert.

" The Chabanais, " as the Parisians call it for shortness, is well organised and carefully managed. The decorations of the rooms are always being renewed and the remount department is kept in full swing, with untiring energy.

There is a sumptuous bath-room, and the principal saloons are arranged in some fancy way, one representing a cabin in a pleasure yacht. Visitors are received in a magnificent hall, modelled from a courtyard of the Spanish Alhambra. An illustrated booklet, giving views of the best appartments, has been issued. Any client can be shown all over this palace of prostitution, if he wishes. There is always one negress, at least, kept on the staff. She is destined for debauchees who may happen to be in mourning, say the jokers of Paris.

The favourites of the seraglio are really very pretty women, of all sizes and colours, to suit every taste.

First, I note Réjane, tall, plump, good-tempered—a jolly girl. Her only sorrow is that she cannot efface the tatooed disfigurement of one of her arms, which by means of hearts, darts, and bold lettering informs all who gaze upon her plump biceps that she belongs " to Ernest for life, " although she has not seen the little pimp, hero of this ineffaceable badge, ever since she was a mere child.

Claudine comes next—thin, saucy, and as playful as a kitten. She greatly resembles Mdlle. Polaire, a well-known actress renowned for her slender figure. Claudine's waist measurement is only 19 inches. By her dashing, sprightly bearing, and even by the cut of her features, she might almost be taken for the twin sister of the famous footlight fairy.

Many playgoers who are fond of the acting and singing of Polaire, queen of the stage, slip round to the lupanar on leaving the theatre, to enjoy the closest intimacy of Claudine of the Chabanais, when with very little imagination, they can, for a small fee, fancy themselves in the deepest embrace of the actress whose presence has just been blotted out of their sight by the fall of the playhouse curtain.

The pick of the brothel basket here is undoubtedly *La Grande Marthe*—Big Martha—as

she is called. A splendid wench; a true type of
the beauties of the Lorraine provinces, with a
Madonna-like, angelic face. Her fair tresses,
soft, silky and long—a most uncommonly beautiful head of hair—form a golden halo, but her
blue eyes are far from being candid, nor are their
glances innocent. Her orbs are of a beautiful
tint, not the dark azure of cornflowers, but
coldly cerulean, like a clear winter sky when the
cutting North winds blow. Beautiful Marthe
is a six-footer, as tall as a horse-guard. In spite
of her commanding stature, her graceful frame
is wonderfully well-proportioned, being both
sturdy, and delicate at the extremities. The
most frigid males, with but slight inclination to
play the game of love, when they set eyes on
lovely Marthe cannot help extolling the
sculptural beauty of this massive living statue.
Always willing to relieve suffering humanity,
she is blessed with an excellent temper, and her
unruffled disposition induces her to lend herself
with equanimity to every possible whim of her
customer—on condition, of course, that he be
kind and polite. She does not get on so well

with those, who seeking brutal pleasure, like to curb a woman beneath their domineering will. When she meets a rough conqueror of this sort, she puts her foot down, soon showing what she is made of, as, under her satin skin, are muscles of steel.

On the other hand, she is an ideal empress for " masochists, " and for all weak beings who love to be humiliated, commanded, ordered about, and badly treated generally by a woman. She drills them according to the desires of their dreams, but while forcing them to execute the most degrading tasks beneath her rod or whip, Marthe can barely keep from smiling.　However, she is so amiable that she manages to remain serious, and play her part to the *dénouement*.

At the Chabanais, the spectacle of living pictures, generally known as *les puces*—the games of the lively flea—is in great vogue.

I need not describe that diversion again, having said all I had to say on this head in a preceding chapter. These *tableaux vivants* are exactly the same in all brothels, and the spasm of love is never real, merely splendidly imitated. It is quite comprehensible that venal sweethearts are not going to give way to the delights of sincere Lesbianism in front of intruding strangers whose sole merit lies in the fact of their being paymasters for the nonce.

Nevertheless, the well-drilled Chabanais charmers go through the postures and groupings of the " lively flea " with vivacious lewdness, their performance finishing in the same farcical way, with the joke about " starch for mother and paste for father. " One girl, also, nevers fails to waddle about the room on all-fours, with a twisted sheet of paper sticking out from between her thighs. She defies her pursuer to light it, and the visitor never succeeds in so doing.

Recently, at this palace of Priapus, there was some talk of erecting a stage. Behind its footlights, beautiful girls were to have danced— fleshings and " tutu " barred. That goes without saying.

Every known lascivious branch of the Terpsichorean art would have been represented ; the true belly-dance, the skirt-dance without drawers, and a waltz of naked women. A hidden orchestra would have accompanied this bawdy ballet, and the spectators, for a consideration, could have afterwards enjoyed any chosen tripping, frisky lass without danger of having his head—or anything else—cut off. In ancient times, when a wench whirled before you, she generally decapitated her tyrant afterwards.

The authorities, when applied to, sternly refused to sanction this saltatory innovation, which, after all, was harmless in every way, especially as all persons entering the brothel take good care to leave shame on the threshold. Such a splendid spectacle, copied from the ancients, would have brought many tourists from far-off lands, and the gayest of cities would have been gayer still.

For amateurs of really natural love-dances, with women tripping the light fantastic toe as Eve very probably did to charm her mate, all in a garden fair—before the fall—I may mention here that such salacious ball-room mysteries may be fully appreciated in the Latin Quarter.

My readers will, I am sure, understand and forgive my regretful reticent prudence, preventing me from publishing the address where the nude ballet is to be seen. If I said any more, I should be giving information to the police.

The Chabanais mansion is sometimes called " the eight-storied house. " The name is deserved, if we include the garrets. Every flat is divided into numerous rooms, neatly furnished in exquisitely correct Louis XV. style, and provided with every sanitary convenience.

The mansion was thrown open in time for the Paris exhibition of 1878, and has flourished ever since. In 1900, when all the inhabitants of the French capital were feverishly awaiting the beneficent shower of foreign gold that was to fill every coffer, the owner of No. 12, Rue Chabanais, with admirable foresight, sold the whole concern—lock, stock, barrel and bidet— for a million of francs (£40.000).

Since then, prices at the Chabanais have gone up. Each successive Exhibition year in Paris is marked by an increase in the tariffs of restaurants and bawdy-houses.

In October, 1900, a fire broke out at the Chabanais, under the roof. It was about eleven o'clock at night and the weather was chilly. The conflagration turned out to be a trifling affair, but it caused a complete panic, the whole staff of caressing lasses rushing into the street in their usual naked state. The drivers on the box-seats of their *fiacres* in the Rue Louvois, where there is a cab-stand, had a grand view, and stray passers-by saw a sight they could never forget. An army of semi-nude sirens in silk brocaded *peignoirs*, muslin wrappers, or even in nothing but transparent, lace-trimmed, gauzy chemises, ran madly hither and thither, dazed, shrieking; dropping into any arms opened to arrest these bewildered beauties in their bird-like flight. The gentlemen visitors had also rushed down the staircase and thence into the streets, without a thought of " adjusting their clothes before leaving. "

Several academical studies of naked males could thus have been made, but the lords of creation looked rather grotesque, shivering in undervests and drawers beneath the biting autumnal breeze of night. The most comical predicament was that of two ladies, wives of notable middle-class tradesmen. These burgess Messalinas had repaired to the Chabanais secret museum to satisfy their private longings. Whether they yearned for Sapphic satisfaction or any other combination, history sayeth not— and becoming panic-stricken in the same way as their less fortunate sisters, fled like them in the same airy undress.

Two years later, another side-splitting scene was caused by the Chabanais crew of venal hussies. It was the National feast-day of the 14th of July. According to custom, a public ball in the open air was held close by, near a drinking-fountain dedicated to the memory of Molière, the famous French playwright.

Bitten by some tarantella-like longing, the Chabanais creatures walked boldly out of doors, in the costume of their nightly commerce—fanciful diaphanous chemise, light wrapper, gaudy hose, high-heeled, coloured satin boots, and naught besides, barring perchance, a cigarette or a fan. Guided by the noise of the blaring band, the painted dames soon found themselves in the midst of the merry crowd of dancers. The joyous stupefaction of the happy polking and perspiring public was soon metamorphosed into entrancing delight when the newly-arrived fairies started a real French eccentric quadrille, garnished with high-kicking of the most unblushing kind, considering that knickers are unknown in a brothel.

Unfortunately, such saturnalia could only last a few minutes in these degenerate days. Soon, our brave guardians of the public peace made their uniformed presence felt. They stood petrified for a second, struck dumb and silly at the unwonted sight. Stifling any excusable concupiscent feelings, they did their duty, but in justice to Paris policemen, I must admit, with manly moderation. Instead of clapping these minxes, as scantily clad as the goddesses of Olympus, whence they seemed to have descended, in a common lock-up, they merely bustled them back to their brothel, and then reported the case to the commissary of the district.

This important functionary was clever enough to confine himself to a severe lecture, which afforded him an excuse for paying a visit next day to the truant trollops, who listened politely, gave signs of repentant emotion, and promised to be good, very good girls for the future.

On leaving the Chabanais palace of prostitution, I have only to walk a few steps before coming to the Rue Sainte Anne, where in the building numbered 37 *bis*, is another house of ill-fame, which may be set down as a burgess brothel.

Quiet, comfortable, but without striking merits, its proprietor has great pretentions and thinks his little temple should rank with the best, because now and then a pretty woman may be picked up therein.

The housekeeper guards her treaures of easy virtue with dragon-like vigilance. She talks loudly and imperiously. Her gestures are redundant and energetic, and she conducts her flock of females and her customers with the same exuberant show of masterful despotism.

There is nothing particular to entice customers to this house—not even the arbitrary manners of its lady manager, so I stroll down the street and shortly find myself in the Rue du Quatre-Septembre. Behind this lordly thoroughfare, running parallel to it, is the Rue de Hanovre. Here, at No. 6, is a large dwelling with all its shutters always closed. This is a fine, well-kept brothel, where my hope of falling on a fresh young piece—some tender chicken—is often fulfilled.

Of course, these little nymphs are not under statutable age, but having only just attained the legal limit when a French woman is allowed to dispose of her body of her own free will. It is true this tolerance is restricted by vile and barbarous bye-laws which sometimes make a philosophical observer doubt if the Gallic people are quite as highly civilised as they flatter themselves to be.

Some nice budding dressmakers may be met with in the reception room of the Rue de Hanovre cathedral of lechery. These are young seamstresses who, after having in vain sought for work all round the neighbourhood, tired of fruitlessly soliciting employment at the principal designers of feminine frippery of the Rue de la Paix, find their tortured entrails clamouring for bread. Ancient prejudice resounds in their ears, murmuring that a woman must remain virtuous at all costs.

Virtue, alas! has never nourished any of its votaries; hypocrisy, on the contrary, may occasionally grant its adepts a square meal.

The starving girl's young brain begins to solve strange social problems. Rendered audacious and brazen by hunger and the perspective of a hot cutlet, the poor sewing maiden remembers the dissolute talk of the workshop and drags her tired feet to the Rue de Hanovre.

After listening to her sad story, a dainty repast is set before her, and when the police regulations have been obeyed, the newcomer is presented to casual clients.

Therefore, it is not to be marvelled at, that a maidenhead may often be found where one would least expect to find it—under the hospitable roof of the Rue de Hanovre home of lust. In such a case, the price asked naturally exceeds the ordinary charge.

When such a curiosity is offered, it is as well not to jump too eagerly at the bargain. It may happen that the proffered rose, this original unopened bud, has already been plucked ; and that what is proposed for sale in glowing language, is merely a second edition, not worth the high price of the real untouched article.

Do not forget that as well as most matrons in other parts of the civilised world, the merry wives of Lutetia know all about the astringent virtues of a concentrated solution of alum.

CHAPTER VIII.

The Temple of the Rue Taitbout.

No. 56, Rue Taitbout is a very old house. Were it not for its hermetically-closed shutters and the sombre hue of the paint covering its stuccoed walls, no one would dream of its being a well-known bordel. Even as it is, there are many busy Parisians who pass it daily and do not know or give a thought to the traffic of human flesh that goes on within its small rooms, reached at the top of a cramped, ancient, stuffy staircase.

Mismanagement and change of fashion has caused this discreet priapic retreat to be forsaken by merrymakers in general, although tourists are frequently taken there by the touts who pester gentlemen—especially those who appear to be strangers to the city—with their whispered offers of service : " Vant a guide, sir? Come and see de bitches, sir? Show you de crystal parlour, sir?" (1)

(1) The following is from the columns of the London " Sporting Times, " October 14, 1905.

" A young American, a few nights ago, accompanied by two companions, paid a visit in the smallest of the hours to a well-known hospitable temple of pleasure of the Rue Taitbout. The presiding goddess was Casque d'Or Golden Helmet so christened on account of her marvellous wealth of yellow hair. She is the friend of a renowned hooligan transported for murder. When her hold-up sweetheart was being examined and tried, this queen of the pavement, for whom the toughs fought and slashed one another in deadly rivalry, was a popular heroine in Paris.

" Cascades of champagne and whiskey were set rolling recklessly, and after three hundred francs' worth of liquors had been paid for, the scantily-clad damsels pressed their gallant visitors to drink again. Soon a fresh bill for more hundreds of francs was presented to the intoxicated youths. One of them, in a fit of mad rage, pulled out a six-shooter and fired. The panic-stricken charmers rushed shrieking into the street, with the exception of Casque d'Or, who had received her baptism of fire when in her teens. The police raided the perfumed saloon, full of tobacco and gunpowder smoke They dragged the silly, drunken young men off to durance vile ; the wounded directress being carried to the hospital, where ineffectual attempts were made to extract a bullet from her shoulder. "

When sober, the defence of the tipsy Yank, who had fired at his hostess, Mademoiselle Eugenie Bass, was that in his own country, after painting the town red, a volley of revolver shots became the obligatory finale to a pleasant evening cowboy fashion. He said he had aimed at a mirror, and the bullet, ricochetting, had unfortunately struck the Lady Superior of the Taitbout Priory

Business in the boudoirs of the Taitbout
stew has dropped of late years. Funds being
low, the furniture has not been furbished up.
The girls on view are far from being first-rate
specimens.

On my last visit here, I fancied myself in some
house of erotic convenience in another land,
where the artistic taste of Paris would be lacking. The lupanars of holy Russia are something like this. It must have been in some such
rough and ready second-class venereal temple of
Venus that the following ukase was issued in
the land of the knout :

REGULATIONS FOR THE NOBLE PUPILS OF THE IMPERIAL MILITARY SCHOOL OF RUSSIA.

1. The licensed brothel, No.—, Street, is exclusively
reserved for the accommodation of the Noble Pupils.

2. Mondays, Tuesdays, and Thursdays are set apart for
the sole use of the Noble Pupils.

3. Visits to the aforesaid house will be made by columns,
viz.

a) Tuesday : the first division of the first squadron.

b) Thursday : the first division of the second squadron.

c) Monday : the second division of the first squadron,
and so on in rotation.

If the number of candidates for admission exceeds that authorised by the present rules, the officer on duty will take such measures as he may deem fitting. On the other hand, vacancies may be filled up by Noble Pupils of the remaining division of the same squadron.

4. From 3 o'clock till 5, on these days, the doctor shall examine the women of the aforesaid house. He must take care that after his examination and before the arrival of the Noble Pupils, the women have no connection with any stranger whatsoever, and that the Noble Pupils do not copulate with any other women than those who have undergone the medical examination.

5. On arriving at the aforesaid house, each Noble Pupil shall be examined by an assistant from the infirmary.

The doctor shall send his report upon the two examinations aforesaid to the officer on duty.

6. On no account shall a woman receive more than three Noble Pupils.

7. The officer on duty shall designate the first pupil to be received by each woman.

8. On no account shall the Noble Pupils be allowed to enter the women's rooms except one at time.

9. The Noble Pupils are not allowed to frequent any other licensed or unlicensed brothel.

10. Each Noble Pupil, on being received by a woman, shall pay 1 rouble, 25 copecks. Under no pretence whatever, can the visit of a Noble Pupil to a woman exceed half-an-hour's duration.

The present regulations will be enforced on and after the 20th of February, 1904.

After this digression, my reader friend may perhaps ask—and with some show of reason—why I reserve a full chapter for the Taitbout house of whoring when I might, had I wished, have devoted a whole volume to pictures and anecdotes of the glorious garden of perfumed lechery in the Rue de Chabanais?

Impatient seeker of truth and light, listen to me. You will soon perceive how after warning you that in these pages you will not find one word of the usual hackneyed descriptions to be discovered timidly touched upon in so-called secret guide-books, I ventured to assert that you will, on the contrary, stumble across many divulgations and useful hints which you may search for in vain elsewhere.

Imagine yourself—now our little misunderstanding is cleared up—in my company. We are standing in the tawdry saloon of the Rue Taitbout house of pleasure. In obedience to the usual call when visitors are announced, all the disengaged recruits of these bawdy barracks have been mustered for our inspection.

See, they are standing before us. Some

throw open their gaudy dressing-gowns, others lift up a single silk petticoat, but all smile and ogle us while they lewdly wriggle the pink tip of a saucy, agile tongue between their painted lips. They writhe snake-like, as if possessed by a demon of lust. This swaying of the body and darting of tongue-tips evoke dreams of serpents in female form, or metamorphosed pythons about to revert to their original form so as to encircle and crush us in their deadly folds. It would be a relief to hear the exhibited creatures hiss. But these poor prostitutes are not allowed to speak. They may show us what they think is the best part of their public bodies—bosom, thigh, leg, or bush—they may pout, mouth, and wink, but that is all. The shameless show of a dozen of nude female slaves offering themselves in silence for hire with the lewdest of lewd gestures may be seen in Paris daily. On the walls of all the public buildings these three words are painted in big letters, " Liberty, Equality, and Fraternity. " The rulers of the Republic who permit and encourage the brothel business ought to add this lavatory label, " For Men Only. "

I am wandering from my subject again, and
the docile doxies are waiting for our verdict.
Look steadfastly at the strumpets, good sir.
They are mostly thin, and of a surety, highly
nervous. They frown; their eyes roll up
and down, and from side to side, with a frightened look, as if they could not control the
movements of their pupils. Their features are
furrowed with deep wrinkles. They seem under the influence of some grave preoccupation,
or profound obsession.

This is because they are all victims to a
fatal, unnatural passion. I find it easy to guess
the nature of the destroying canker, indigenous
to the neurotic environment of the crapulous
cloister. It is not gambling, alcohol, or mor-
phine. It is love.

Love, radiant love; heartfelt affection?
Are you joking?—asks my sceptical and impatient reader friend.

I am perfectly serious, or as serious as I can
be. Please note, however, that I have not yet
specified what kind of love I allude to.

These women of the Taitbout are ardent,

furious *tribades*. They have been carefully selected among women who love their own sex and designedly so.

If this house of orgies does not appeal to its visitors by luxurious fittings ; if it seems neglected, the real reason is because the ordinary customer, wishing for cheap and rapid relief from erotic influence, is not wanted here.

Rich and eccentric *blasé* rakes are alone catered for ; men whose brains are full of haunting visions of impossible lust ; men who are willing to pay large sums for extraordinary refinements of voluptuousness, in attempts to rouse their worn-out lust or realise their dreams of lascivious nightmare manias.

It costs dear to witness the bacchanalia of the " lively flea " beneath this roof of randiness, but the sum asked is proportionate to the display, which in this instance is real.

When the witches are intertwined in the unblushing ceremony of their Sapphic sabbath, one hears genuine moans of real love, sighs of intense joy, cries of pleasure, groans of painful ecstasy escaping from the hoarse throats of the

lewdest Lesbians in the world, closely embracing in the salacious anguish of the vilest,
wild sexless kisses.

Their movements are quite different to those
of the damsels I have seen at other brothels.
When a girl first approaches her delighted partner in the Sapphic Taitbout tournament, the
preliminary caresses are full of tender solicitude, quite maternal, reminding the spectator of
an affectionate mother fondling a favourite
daughter. The sight of such ineffable devotion
becomes almost chaste.

Little by little, a wave of lurid passionate
yearning sweeps through the throbbing brains
of the naked couple. They press their fleshy
frames together, bosom to bosom; two fleecy
triangles mingling as their eager hands wander
with brutal, rapid mutual touchings. They
wrestle together. The tentacles of their vile
yearning grips them tightly. Kisses are followed by love-bites. Fondling fingers now
scratch and tear; cat-like claws starting from
their velvet paws.

With feline wriggling, these tigresses stuggle

in a hot embrace and beads of perspiration start on their skin. The fragrant scent floating in the air of the brilliantly-lighted room changes, becoming heavier, and the odour of female seething sex mounts to the nostrils of the rutting looker-on.

The worn-out women pant and strive. They are fighting to reach the fearful goal of tribadic supreme enjoyment; to conquer the resistance of their overwrought bodies, forcing their vibrating nerves to carry them to the point of spermatic exhaustion—that summit of voluptuous upheaval whence they quickly fall again, never assuaged, never satisfied; doomed to try and glut their insensate craving eternally, without ever being able to entirely appease their relentless depraved appetite.

The revelation of this female sexual inversion is grotesque. At the same time, oddly enough, a little pity and respect swells up within me, banishing the mocking laugh that was rising to my lips.

In order to assist at these diabolical diversions, inquisitive ladies moving in the best circles come to the Taitbout disguised in masculine attire. Sometimes, they are not content to remain simple spectatresses, but join in the sports.

A thinker, philosopher, or student of psychology noting and reflecting upon the varied manifestations of sexual instinct, finds not only amazement and amusement in watching these scenes of debauchery driven to its utmost limits, but he also deduces great moral lessons therefrom.

What they be it is not my province to determine here. I leave such serious meditation to the intelligent consideration of any broad-minded man or woman knowing how poor humanity is after all at the mercy of the cannonade of carnal desire for ever beseiging our weak understanding.

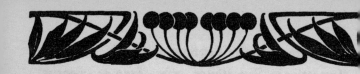

CHAPTER IX.

From the Gare de l'Est
to the Big Boulevards.

The Boulevard de Strasbourg, the Rue Saint-Denis and the big Boulevards from the Porte Saint Denis to the Porte Saint Martin constitute the domain of actors and variety performers—" the profession," as it is styled in Great Britain, reigning supreme in this part of the joyous town.

In every *café* of this quarter can be seen the blue-chinned players, accompanied by their female companions with peroxide tresses and powdered features. They play cards or dominoes, gesticulating, telling their lying tales, striking attitudes, and ordering a glass of beer with the gestures of the King drinking to Hamlet.

Here and there perchance a pretty woman's face or graceful figure may shine out among many down-at-heel tragedy queens or cheap music-hall " serio-comic " ladies, but these actresses and cantatrices are not alluring either by their looks, dowdy dress, or melodramatic bearing.

But my present task is to write about those women who sit patiently indoors waiting for their adorers to come to them—bedecked idols in closed temples.

The lives and loves of the pretty little actresses of Paris would furnish ample matter for many sturdy volumes. Books as big as Bibles could be written round the music-halls ; their staff on the stage and their friends in the stalls—vice on the boards ; ladies for ladies, men for men, with catamites and the queens of Lutetia-Lesbos waiting at the stage exit.

This part of Paris is full of lecherous trade and loving intrigue. To describe it fully, life would be too short. I am not editing an Encyclopædia Gallica of gallantry. My little book is naught but an album of sensual sketches. It is not a vast gallery of finished pictures of prostitution.

Crossing the Boulevard, I find myself in the Boulevard Sébastopol—the " Sébasto, " according to Paris slang—where the street-walker and her inevitable pimp hold high revel.

Had I not sworn to digress no more, I would devote a few pages to cheap beerhouses in these parts. They are wretched *cafés*, know as *vacheries*—cow-houses—because women serve the clients. There are almost as many of these establishments as in the Latin Quarter, and their only attraction is the faded beauty of the waitresses, often in fancy costumes.

In former days, it was impossible to walk in the streets without seeing closed shutters suddenly opened and held ajar, allowing a stroller to get a vague glimpse of some enchanting female form, which melted again in the shadow after a white hand had been thrust forth—beckoning.

Through the efforts of virtuous police regulations, the pink fingers of invitation are no longer flourished, although in certain parts near here, such as the Faubourg Saint Martin and the Rue des Petites Ecuries this old-world custom still exists.

In these two streets, full of genuine, busy traders, there are two houses facing each other, where three or four obliging ladies of the second floor carry on this system of calling their customers from the street, from ten in the morning until five in the evening. This is, after all, a branch of brothel life and therefore comes within my field of observation.

I knew a young creature, a real Parisienne, born at Belleville, who earned her living in this way. She had the smallest foot I ever saw. Friquette was her name. She was a babbling baby, full of childish talk and silvery song. Poor little Friquette Sit-by-the-Window, where art thou now?

As they are carried on in the year of grace 1906, the houses of the Faubourg Saint Martin are not worthy of being visited or sampled.

I do not say this for No. 72, in the Rue du

Château d'Eau which stands head, shoulders and bosom above the bagnios of this locality.

If you go to the house I have just quoted, take care which staircase you ascend, as there are several. Get your bearings from the street by looking up at the first floor. You will see the windows, garnished with tasty silk blinds. They are a poem in themselves and serve as a significant signboard in such a dingy business neighbourhood.

It is one of the best bagnios in Paris. First and foremost, the girls are all pretty. It is true that the youngest is well over twenty-one, the legal limit, but the eldest is not more than twenty-five.

Do not forget to admire the housekeeper or directress—call her what you will. She is in the full bloom of maturity—thirty-five years of age at the most. But what a finely made female, as upright as a dart! Her features are surprisingly regular and well-cut. She has the massive head of the Roman matron or the figurative Republic of France, always symbolically pictured as a fine woman. Or I may venture to say that her profile is like that seen on antique Grecian medals, so much admired by artists.

I admire her too. And so will you, reader, when you see her. That is what I go to brothels for—to admire female beauty and study it as closely as I can.

Such a charming directress of a well-ordered house of joy was never known. She is charming, and understands a man and his desires from top to toe—with stoppages in between.

It is useles to court her. She will tell you what she informed your scribe—that she has retired from active service and is now content to drill new recruits instead of taking up arms herself.

To prove her words, she left the room and returned three minutes later, driving before her one of her little lambs, a blonde angel with an innocent air. The tempting minx looked for all the world like an engraved demure beauty from a "Keepsake" album of 1830, and the illusion was kept up by old-fashioned golden corkscrew curls clustering on either side of the pure oval of her tiny features.

To entice me, the cunning and affable presiding matron draws aside the dressing-gown which is the angel's only attire, and calls my attention to the winsome lassie's wee extremities, small waist, flat and polished ivory belly, two tiny breasts like little apples, and the soft tuft of glittering yellow down hiding her pink mark of sex.

We go off with her. When I say " we," I mean that I can no longer resist. Besides, I do not want to vex the directress who has so kindly fetched this fair flower for me. Madame is so grateful and pleased that she swears she will remain while I enjoy the plump bird of paradise. So I follow her as she leads her girl by the hand. That is what I meant by " we."

Soon the three of us are in a cosy bedroom, clean and inviting. Faithful to her promise, the mistress of the house does not leave me, and brings the weight of her experience and all her sensual science to supplement the awkward efforts of my bride of an hour who is quite a novice. By a host of delicate little attentions all conducive to the conclusion of my amatory duel, Madame leads me on to almost perfect ravishment.

I am undressed on the bed. The young lass with the golden locks is by my side in the same condition. We are Adam and Eve, lazily reclining in the garden of Eden. The directress is the serpent. She tempts us to sin— several times—enfolding us in her clever caresses.

Dost like the picture? The delight is rare, and a path of roses conducts me to the inevitable apotheosis of Nature, by means of long drawn-out acute sweet agony,

Nothing could be more delicious than this scene of an Elder between two Susannahs, and it only cost me one louis. When I handed over the miserable twenty-franc piece, I was heartily thanked over and over again.

Decidedly Paris is synonymous with Paradise. Oh, thrice blessed town—beloved of cities!

One within its walls, the stranger must find his way about alone and ask nothing of anybody. Beware of guides; they are expensive, and know nothing of the secrets of the streets and alleys.

At No. 72, Rue du Château d'Eau, you are not worried or pestered. You are also in perfect safety. I was not pressed to drink or spend money. Have a bottle of champagne, if you like ; or order nothing — you will be treated with the same respect. The women there are taught not to pull dolent faces, or to make clucking noises with their wicked tongues against the roofs of their mercenary mouths. Such suggestive mimicry signifies the throes of thirst all the world over.

Regretfully leaving this hall of ejaculation, I step over in a twinkling to the Cité Jarry, a passage with a gateway, formerly a celebrated corner for copulation,

In those days at nightfall, strumpets carried on their casement commerce with impunity. From behind half-closed shutters gleamed mysterious rays of light, furnished by lamps with pink shades. Women were on the watch for the footfalls of wandering lechers.

When I passed, one side of the shutter

would be pushed back against the wall with a sharp snap. Mechanically, the man in the street looked up and saw the priestress of Priapus lean forward. The figure of the female seemed finely-proportioned, contrasting against the glowing red background of the lighted rosy room. The scarlet woman's features were pretty, and there was a momentary pleasing glimpse of a rounded white arm emerging from the loose lace-trimmed sleeve of a light-coloured dressing-gown.

Nowadays, no graceful vision bursts upon the wayfarer's enraptured gaze. The mystery and poetry of such apparitions are out of date.

In this prosaic age, the brutality of the brothel alone remains, with all the realism of its sensuous crudity.

There are two houses of ill-fame in the Cité Jarry. The business of both is carried on in the first-floor flat.

There is nothing, however, to encourage me to describe them more fully.

It suffices for me to tell you, once for all, that the boarders in these second-rate brothels are nearly all drawn from the serried ranks of the night-walkers treading the asphalte pavement of the Boulevard Sébastopol, near the Rue Quincampoix, or ceaselessly walking up and down the Faubourg Montmartre between the Rue Geoffroy-Marie and the Rue Cadet. They are well-worn whores between twenty-five and thirty, generally stout morsels.

Fat women are mostly indolent and lean unknowingly towards bawdy-house monotony, because their innate lazy nature causes them to feel all abroad when their lovers leave them, or are in prison.

In such a plight, a strumpet with this disposition seeks refuge in the sanctuary of a stew, returning to the hazards of street prostitution when she finds a fresh master.

A thin wench, with highly-strung nerves, is much more active; valiant and energetic when in trouble of this kind, and being independent, prefers her liberty above all things.

CHAPTER X.

The Rue Laferrière, with a Few Words about the Flagellants of the Rue Clauzel.

Starting from the open Place Saint-Georges is a street which is hardly of any use, for it winds round and finishes without a break in the Rue Bréda, now Rue Henri Monnier, near the Rue Notre-Dame-de-Lorette. The Rue Laferrière is the name of this thoroughfare, built in days when mysterious whims seemed to inspire municipal architects and surveyors.

When I say that the Rue Laferrière is devoid of practical utility, I am in error. As the mass of traffic passes through the Place Saint-Georges and the Rue Notre-Dame-de-Lorette, the quaint curved row of houses serves as a quiet retreat for pedestrians stricken with love-hunger. The street is an ideal site for brothels.

Formerly it was full of these temples of rapid pleasure. Women stood on every threshold, or gibbered at all the windows. In our sober epoch there are three brothels, all quite ordinary and with no redeeming or striking features.

So I will pass on and devote my time to exploring the Rue Clauzel, which is quite near.

Unfortunately, the inquisitive Parisian police have also been making discoveries in this neighbourhood. There is no peace or rest nowadays for honest fornicators. Thieves and hooligans are alone left undisturbed. They operate at their ease, getting away unmolested with our watches and purses, while the Sherlock Holmes gentry of the French capital devote all the energy they possess to interfering with the pleasures of Parisian voluptuaries.

If I make so bold as to growl at our guardians of public safety, it is that you may excuse

me for not being able to set down here where
the interesting Confraternity of Flagellants
now holds its meetings.   During the year 1904,
these brethren of the birch foregathered in
a house situated Rue Clauzel, until they
were hunted down, harried, and obliged to
disperse.

This much can I say, without betraying
any secrets that may put detectives on the track
of flogging friends : my readers will find them
in this neighbourhood.

Every libertine knows that man as he reaches
the highest pinnacle of progress, also tries to
improve his sensual sensations and render them
more perfect.   These proceedings of refinement always displease the authorities who
declare such efforts immoral, and consequently
harmful ; a crime against the commonwealth.

Without venturing in these pages upon arguments where I could easily show I was right,
but which would perhaps savour of anarchy,
I will only declare audaciously that let legislators
do as they will, he who seeks for extra special
priapic joys will never be satisfied with the

ordinary tame process of manufacturing children in the arms of his legitimate spouse. If the brain of a bold burgher be undermined by lascivious longings, inducing him to wallow in out-of-the-way venery, he will obtain the satisfaction of which he dreams, come what may.

Among the strangest passions that rack our being is a very common one known as " sadism, " although it has swayed humanity's genital gymnastics long before the Marquis de Sade—from whose name this term is derived— came into the world.

It was at the end of the last century that the depraved French nobleman wrote about the voluptuous delights of cruelty, but to be logical we ought to seek for the source of pleasure-pain in ancestral habits, developed from an atmosphere of uncivilised environment. Prehistorical man, in woods and forests, when marriage had not yet become a holy alliance, hunted a coveted woman in the same way as he sought to capture or kill any living beast or bird.

The woman was sore afraid. Even if not timid, she fled all the same, inspired by the coquetry of her passive disposition. When run down by the rutting male exasperated by his yearning and the ardour of the pursuit, she was in all likelihood rather roughly treated. This savage behaviour pleased her greatly, if I judge by the preference so many women show for men who rule them with a rod of iron.

Be this as it may, I merely make the foregoing cursory remarks to preface the story I have to tell showing how an intelligent procuress assisted those voluptuaries who look upon flagellation as a sacred rite and whose senses are never appeased unless their female pleasure-toys are well flogged as an appetiser before sacrificing to Venus.

The meretricious and complaisant go-between opened a brothel, Rue Clauzel, in an apartment admirably situated for the purpose, being at the back of a big house, at the end of a courtyard. The door of the saloon, where the birching discipline was applied, was carefully padded, and to reach it, it was necessary to pass through a long corridor where the walls were thickly tapestried. There were also heavy curtains intercepting and deadening any cries or suspicious sounds which might have led uninitiated eavesdroppers to fancy that unwilling victims were being ill-treated.

In this flat were many other rooms, no different from ordinary bawdy-house bedchambers, except that they were abundantly garnished with layers of quilted stuffs on wainscoting and ceiling. These snuggeries were used by amateurs of the birch whe liked to indulge their peculiar propensity in private, shut in with the goddess of their choice.

Having thus completed the arrangements of her whipping palace, the procuress soon found means to put her hands upon many young women having no objection to let themselves be fustigated.

She went to Belleville and Montmartre, and whenever she met any saucy baggage who seemed suitable for the purpose of having her fat young bottom scarified, the enterprising matron would address her in the following way, using persuasive speeches much to this effect :

" You are a silly goose, my dear, to let yourself be thrashed and beaten black and blue by your fancy man who'll stab or disfigure you one of these fine days. How will you look then ? Instead of handing over all you earn to a lazy rascal in exchange for showers of blows—his only liberality—wouldn't you be better off earning a tremendous lot of money by allowing yourself to be birched ? Besides, my love, half the time, it's only for fun and don't hurt a bit. You can but try just for once, and if you don't like it, you needn't continue. We shan't kill you."

Many girls refused ; others accepted. Once in the comfortable brothel, they all elected to remain.

With blushing reticence, I will now try and describe, as faithfully as my halting pen will permit me, one of the memorable flagellating orgies I was privileged to witness, and which, in spite of all the brutal raids and intrusions of the police, I am convinced will always take place in some part of Paris.

At nine o'clock at night, I ascended the hilly streets reaching to the heights of Montmartre, and bearing off towards a street on my right, arrived at my destination. A staircase had to be mounted, and then the procuress came forward to receive me, smiling her stereotyped commercial smile, while her eyes glistened with a glance of suspicion. She did not know me.

Taking me for a common type of unsophisticated lecher, she starts by trying to introduce me to one of the most insignificant members of her bawdy battalion.

" Has the ceremony began, madame ? " I ask, taking off my hat to her in my best Sunday manner, with exaggerated respect. " I should be sorry if I'm late ! "

She tries to feign surprise and laughs loudly, seeing that whatever I am, I am certainly not a police spy. So she becomes more amiable, happy after all to recruit a fresh amateur of birching lust.

" We've been waiting for you, my dear sir!" she runs on, entering into the spirit of the joke. " We couldn't very well commence without you, could we now ? Ha! ha! But you must let me announce your arrival to your brother birchers. I shan't be a second. Sit down in that armchair. There—in front of that pane of glass. That's right ! Don't move, and look pleasant—as the photographing chaps say. I'll return in a few minutes to fetch and introduce you ! "

She is gone, leaving me alone in a little, brilliantly-lighted entrance-hall. In front of me is a hole in the wall with a square of glass let in, masked by a gauze curtain hanging on the other side where all is dark.

Should my reader ever find himself in such a position, he must not be uneasy. I am not. I have been told to remain perfectly quiet. I know why. The lady of the house has simply gone to warn the members of the whipping club that a newcomer solicits the honour of admission. These worthy gentlemen have no wish to be compromised, so before consenting to receive me in their midst, they want to see if I am worthy, and what I look like. That is why I remain steadfast and unmoved, with the strong glare of electricity beating on my face while the whole birching band passes in turn before the glass window in the adjoining darkened room. I cannot see them, but they can see me. If their verdict is against me, I shall certainly not be allowed to view their flogging festival.

Such is the plain and logical explanation of my mysterious reception. I can perfectly well comprehend that the wielders of the rod do not care to admit the first-comer to their castigating circle. These scruples are a guarantee for me—simple spectator.

I must have passed favourably through the ordeal of inspection, for here comes the lady of the house, her features wreathed in kindly smiles.

" Pray follow me, " she says sweetly.

I willingly obey and reap the reward of my patience at once, for the sight that suddenly breaks in upon my gaze is curious and unique.

Eight gentlemen are seated in a spacious saloon. The vast room is illuminated with dazzling brilliancy, and its walls are simply hung with dark red cloth. This sombre crimson background enhances the lily-white nakedness of eight young women, who, in the simple costume of Eve, stand in modest and submissive attitudes before the assembled men.

One of the girls is perched on a high chair, so lofty that the bewitching lass's feet do not reach to the floor. She has an open book on her knees, and is laboriously trying to spell some difficult words, while a gentleman in correct evening dress stands by her side.

He is doubtless her teacher. He has a pair of thick grey whiskers—are they false? — and listens attentively to her ineffectual attemps at spelling. He does not appear to be pleased with her progress, if I may judge by the enormous paper dunce's cap surmounting her abundant locks.

Another beautiful young wench is on her knees. At intervals she bends forward and kisses the patent-leather boots of a gentleman, seemingly so deeply absorbed by his own thoughts that he pays no attention to the maiden in this humiliating posture.

His indifference is feigned, belied by the smile of proud satisfaction lighting up his austere features every time he feels the woman's lips pressed on his boot, thereby giving fresh proofs of her abjection.

A little farther on, a splendidly-proportioned dark nymph stands erect in all the radiant beauty of her absolute nudity, her arms stretched out horizontally to right and left. She forms the figure of a cross, and in front of her is a middle-aged man, a smart frockcoat tightly buttoned over his swelling stomach.

He carelessly fingers a riding-whip, which he causes to hiss through the air, now and again. Each time his victim shows signs of fatigue, forcing her to lower her rosy, plump arms, he flourishes the cutting switch over her head. At this threatening gesture, she gives a little frightened shriek. Up go her arms again, stiffly held out, more straight than ever.

A perfect picture of a thin, immature girlie

who seems not more than sixteen years of age—in reality she is twenty-three, but these miracles may be often noticed among poor-blooded *Parisiennes*—is zealously cleaning the boots of a man who indolently puffs at an obese, gartered cigar, while the poor little creature tries hard to force the rebellious surface of the leather to shine.

All the other women, without a rag to their shapely backs, are in the same postures of slavish humiliation, mastered by these elegantly-dressed men of fashion. I may call this spectacle, " the game of female service. " All these angelic obedient beauties, carrying themselves humbly, minister to their masters' domineering lust. The male conquerors have a haughty bearing, as if they entertained lofty ideas concerning their own value, certain of their superiority, and delighted because these women bow down before them.

So far, the sport is harmless, almost childish. But there must be a sequel, I thought. And so there was. The storm I expected soon burst.

The professor began the tempest. His pretty pupil, with true or feigned awkwardness, perhaps forming part of the evening's programme, suddenly dropped her book. It fell from her lap to the ground.

Her teacher, greatly enraged, declared in stentorian tones that she should be punished. Prayers, tears, and lamentations had no effect. He was inflexible. Harshly but firmly, as becomes a pedagogue, he ordered her to rise from her chair and go down on her knees in the middle of the room, where before everybody —'' in front of the whole class,'' he exclaimed, '' I'll give you a good birching ! ''

With clasped hands, in vain the ill-fated girl cries that she will never do it again, never be naughty any more.

'' Pardon, pardon ! '' she implores in heart-rending accents, and sobbing in a way that almost moves me to tears.

Her inexorable schoolmaster pushes her before him to the middle of the room.

She falls on her knees, and every eye devours the secrets of her trembling nudity. Again she lifts her tightly-joined hands with tender appeals for pity. Her master now grasps a bunch of long, supple twigs of fine ripe birch, neither too fresh nor too dry. There is no danger of the carefully-selected lithe branches snapping or breaking. They are too flexible and elastic.

Many of the members of this flagellating fraternity are Russians, and the rods come from Saint-Petersburg. It is said that the best birch in the world grows in Russia.

The instrument of torture I saw was elegantly arranged. It was composed of a slender packet of long slim branches, fastened together at the thick end by a pink silk bow, with a bunch of streaming ribbons at the side. These gay strips of various hues wind and whirl at the least movement in quite a pleasing way.

Meanwhile, the master, very solemn and dignified, looks through his half-closed lids at his handsome pupil, enjoying her mad terror so much that he is in no hurry to deal the first blow.

" Do you repent, wretched girl ? " he asks

her. " Are you not ashamed of your abominable indolence ? "

" Oh yes ! " she tearfully responds. " Pity ! I beseech you—do please forgive me ! "

" If I pardoned you, you would never improve. You must be birched. Punishment has become a necessity. It is for your good. This time, there will be no weakness on my part. Not an iota of the deserved correction shall be remitted. You recollect how you suffered last Friday ? That was a full week ago, and I can still see the marks on your immodest bottom. That flogging, mademoiselle, although severe enough, is nothing compared to what I have in reserve for you at present. I intend you never to forget it ! "

" Oh ! pardon me ! Don't hurt me ! " groaned the wretched damsel, dazed with fear.

She threw her arms round her ferocious master's legs, and like a nun kissing a crucifix, the weeping maiden pressed her lips to his knees and thighs.

He cast her from him roughly ; then seizing her by the nape of the neck, bent her down towards the floor. She was on all-fours, her vast and firm posteriors jutting out ; the skin of the rosy rump tightly stretched.

It was a most charming posture, artistically suited to the sculptural grace of her perfect female form. She was thin, but sufficiently well covered with firm, pink flesh, full of dimples ; especially on the two globes of her hinder charms, now puckered into goose-flesh through fright.

Her professor smiled grimly, as his victim shrieked with all her might. Her cries were strident and hoarse ; mingled with convulsive moans and sobs.

I could quite understand why she howled and yelled. Her sufferings must have been terrible, her tormentor being true to his word. He slashed at her splendid posteriors unmercifully, according to his promise, and never thought to spare her for an instant.

His rod whistled through the air like the wind in a gale at sea through the yards of a sailing vessel struggling in a tempest. Down came the murderous sharp ends of the birch ; cut

quickly succeeding cut, and the beautiful rosy
flesh, taking on mother-o'-pearl tints beneath
the electric lamps, was soon covered with livid
weals.

The executioner continued unmoved, slowly
and scientifically striking at the tortured twin
hemispheres that were now streaked with a
marbled pattern of blue, dark brown, and thin
red scratches and dots.

I said he thrashed the girl " scientifically."
I use this term with due deliberation, because
I would have my reader know that flagellation
is a science and an art, at one and the same
time.

The false schoolmaster struck quickly.
Stroke followed stroke swiftly, yet each successive, stinging cut was laid on methodically.
Never did the spreading ends of the sharp rod
fall twice on the same spot. Without this
precaution of refined cruelty, the bruised skin,
of such a fine texture, would have been broken,
and blood would have flowed ; useless bar-
barity, which might eventually have been
fraught with grave danger.

Sometimes he would even assault his victim's

calves, and nothing was more deliciously exhilarating than to see the girl's naked legs writhing and struggling beneath the sudden, unexpected onslaught, unless it was the undulation of her backside when the birch bit into the swollen, smarting flesh.

The flogging fiend now changed his position. He had been standing by his pupil's side with one hand weighing heavily on the back of her neck.

He now stood in front of her, and clasped her head between his legs. The wretched wench knew by sad experience what she would now have to endure, so howls of despair burst from her, while she drew in the martyred cheeks of her backside as tightly as she could, closing, too, her reddened thighs.

Her paltry attempts at defence were quite ineffectual, as her torturer bent down, and still maintaining her head between his knees, he seized one of her legs, drew it apart with a strong pull, and dashed his fearful bunch of birch into the dark opening where nestled the secret coral grotto of her sex.

Things were getting tragically serious, I

thought, as I heard the horrible unearthly shriek that the poor martyred slut gave in reply to this attack. I felt deeply stirred. It was all I could do to restrain myself from rushing to her assistance.

I had forgotten that the upward swinging cut was the supreme artifice of true flagellants—the crowning-point of their lascivious torture, without which all their work would be useless and barren, productive of no resulting reciprocal lubricity on the part of the female victim.

The seeming cruelty of flagellants arises from a highly refined trick of voluptuousness. They reason rightly when they say that in persons of neurotic temperament, pleasurable sensations circle in waves of lewd enjoyment— acute delight with an admixture of fleshly suffering and excruciating pain, following upon the enchanting preludes of disrobing before a man, and the passive fascination of giving way to the indecent commands of an overbearing lover.

By reason of her mental and physical inferiority, the woman is in ecstasies at feeling herself completely at the mercy of a strong man. Terror causes her to look upon him with the greatest respect, and this fear, which permeates her entire being, is not without procuring agreeable vibrations to her jarring nerve-centres.

But when the lash attains the most sensitive spot in her whole body, the pain is promptly metamorphosed into sensuous longings. That is why expert girl-whippers, well aware of the effect of such intense, insidious wonder-working pain, always call it to their aid at the close of their copious discipline.

The suffering minx being let free, rose quickly to her feet. Propelled by the inward prompting movement of rising lust, she rushed forward as swiftly as a bolt from a catapult.

For a moment, I thought that blinded by rage or a desire for immediate revenge, the victim was about to throw herself on her torturing flogger, trying to tear his eyes out or strangle him.

I was entirely mistaken, and could hardly

believe my eyes when I saw her overwhelm him with the wildest caresses. It was a relief to me to see how, while her own eyes were still wet with tears, she rained kisses on his stern orbs. Then she licked his cheeks, and her rosy tongue played madly round his neck and ears.

She was in a wild frenzy and ardently longed to be loved, taken, and fully enjoyed by her whilom tormentor, finally gluing her hot lips to the mouth of the man who had so cruelly cut her bum to pieces. It was a never-ending kiss of mad, feverish lust. As she thrust her tongue into her master's mouth, she arched her body backwards in throes of lewd joy while only the whites of her eyes could be seen.

The triumphant birching gentleman led her away. Overcome by delicious lassitude, she leant upon him, as if the mere fact of being half carried in his arms sufficed to open the secret sluices of her inmost enjoyment.

The pair did right to retire at that psychological moment. There are certain instants in life by which we should profit, for they rarely occur twice.

The other gentlemen continue their fun, varying their birching pastimes. I was lucky enough on this occasion to see the flogging dance, or birching races—most gay and laughter-provoking.

The remaining seven flagellants becoming passive spectators, retired to the wall, standing close to it in line, after the naked girls had cleared away chairs and every bit of furniture.

A signal being given, the naked slaves, each armed with a be-ribboned, wicked-looking birch-rod, began to chase each other, trying to strike a bottom, and by running away and dodging not be struck in return. When a shapely arm, brandishing the fatal birch, is in close proximity to a companion's plump backside beauties—down it comes! The panting, laughing hussies cut each other's hinder charms with strength and skill, but generally awkwardly enough.

With loud cries and shrill laughter, the pursuit continues. Breasts rise and fall, shaken by the effort of sprinting to avoid punishment. Splendid vistas of the deepest recesses of the female form are afforded; pink clefts gaping in the midst of thick undergrowth ; sepia crannies flashing into the light for an instant between blushing buttocks covered with scratches, bruises and tiny drops of blood, from blows of the birch bestowed haphazard. Arms, thighs, loins, rosy faces, gleaming eyes, streaming locks—a vision of fitful, ripe beauty ; a dream of enchanting divine bodies, built for man's enjoyment and recklessly displayed in a thousand incessant changes of entrancing, artless, graceful postures.

A girl strikes another. Her momentary victim howls with pain, clapping one hand to her injured bum-cheek. The minx who dealt the succesful stinging cut bursts out laughing, and is so delighted that she forgets to keep a lookout behind her. Chastised in her turn, her gloating guffaw changes to a sharp yelp of agony, and smarting with rage, she turns on her assailant. All strike in turn, and retributive justice overtakes the striker. So the game goes on.

They are out of breath and stop from sheer

fatigue. There is not a bum which not is scarlet; some are mangled and gored out of all knowledge.

Every man claims a favourite perspiring pet. The senses of the male torturers and panting female sufferers have been exacerbated to the highest pitch. Each couple seeks sensual satisfaction and retire to private rooms.

I am alone, somewhat bewildered; vexed at being alone without some perfumed light of love to keep me company and assuage my desires aroused by the birching scenes I have just witnessed.

Luckily for me, one of the flagellators, feeling slightly unwell after so much excitement, departs for home, leaving a young brunette— she who was forced to kiss the boots of a Mere Brute—without a male animal to put out the fires kindled in her womb by the birching games of the night.

Madame proposes that I should console her. Nothing loth, I am conducted to the boudoir where my naked charmer, gasping, hot, and with burning bum, lies rolling on a low couch.

She was ripe for the act of propagation. I should like to describe the ravishing state she was in, but can only find a rather vulgar simile. Imagine a juicy steak hissing on the gridiron, the gravy starting from its rosy cells, waiting to be taken from the fire—and devoured.

I was hungry, and did my duty. She was a fitting partner, and I had no repugnance when, in our delicious spasms of unbridled lust, the pulpy vermilion lips that had been pressed to dusty boots adhered to my moustache as if they would never leave my mouth again.

Under these circumstances, my reader will no doubt pardon me if I draw a veil over the concluding exercises of this memorable night of enjoyment. We shall meet again—in the next chapter.

CHAPTER XI.

Mélanie, the Man-Tamer.

I am conceited enough to fancy that my description of the Flagellating Club, with its members in full working order, has pleased you, oh most gentle of readers?

Of course it did! I beg therefore to announce that the next set of pictures in my concupiscent cinematograh of Cupid's vagaries will show you the other side of the medal.

It is quite impossible that you had never before heard of men whose great delight lies in humiliating womankind, causing tender, trembling maidens to suffer. Now that you see such strange birching males do exist, your next step is to try and realise that there are others who experience quite as much rapture in being brow-beaten by a pet in petticoats.

Both these categories of erotomaniacs pass their lives — the hidden part of their existence — in the insensate pursuit of a will-o'-the-wisp, a meretricious mirage, fading away on the horizon of their daydreams of debauchery directly they seem to attain the illusory goal.

A disciple of the Marquis de Sade, an amateur of cruelty. may perhaps satisfy his vile longing to a certain extent, or even gorge himself completely with bloodthirsty lust, if he be bold enough to brave the severity of just laws edicted to restrain vampires and Jack-the-Rippers.

On the other hand, the " masochist, " or women's slave, goes through life from youth to old age, seeking to realise the fictions of his disordered faculties. Despite all his humility, and the servile cult he pays the female into whose hands he delivers himself as lackey to her lusts, he never finds the ideal queen his imagination has set up upon a visionary throne. All the laws of Nature are opposed to his system of masculine subjection.

In the foregoing chapter, I pointed out that
sadism was a retrogression of the sexual instinct, or rather an unusual persistance of here-
dity; a return to the epoch when man tracked a
female through virgin forests, throwing himself
upon his quarry like a wild stallion overtaking a
mare, to leap upon her, bite her neck and satisfy
lustful longings, while the chosen mate shies
and kicks to rid herself of her agressor.

All lewd inversions, however hideous, can be
explained—nay, even excused—except that of
" masochists. " It remains unaccountable.
Yet it flourishes, being much more common
than might be imagined.

By her feeble physical conformation and the
yielding sweetness of her disposition, a woman
cannot grasp the meaning of the man who
appears to her asking to be beaten, outraged,
and made to suffer at her hands. If she con-
sents and makes up her mind to ill-treat her
servile lover, she goes timidly to work and can
hardly keep from laughing.

Nevertheless, although a rarity and almost
always actuated by thoughts of lucre, the Tamer
of Men is to be found in this worn-out globe

of ours, and in Paris, too—the brightest of cities where everything can be had, especially in the domain of love and passion.

A tyrannical charmer who revels in reigning over the so-called lords of the creation, knocking them about like so many puppets, or trampling them ruthlessly beneath her high heels is to be found in a licensed brothel, comfortable, and properly organised, No. 43, Rue de la Lune, at the corner of the Rue Poissonnière.

On arriving within its cosy reception saloon, I ask to see Mélanie. The reply is that everybody wants Mélanie ! She is making the fortune of the house. I have to wait my turn, as that lady is—ahem !—" in hand."

I resign myself to a long spell of waiting and order a bottle of champagne, just to pass away the time.

Accompanying the wine, come two desirable demireps, whose eyes, with glistening, painted lids and lashes, sparkle when the housekeeper obeys my orders. It is not often that a visitor demands " fizz " without being cajoled into calling for it. So the pair of naked whores smile upon me tenderly, with the caressing expression due to all moneyed worshippers at their shrine.

I am visiting this haunt of pleasure to make notes for the shocking book you are now reading, so I can loll in my armchair unconcernedly and wait to interview Mélanie. In the meantime, I do not see why I should refrain from making a thorough investigation of the charms of the two litle she-devils who offer themselves to me with an entire and refreshing lack of pudicity.

The two young persons agree that I talk to them like an amusing man of the world, who also knows how to handle their exposed charms pleasantly and skilfully. Inwardly flattered by such testimony to my talents of conversation and hidden experience in the science of sensuality, I might have carried my explorations to the uttermost limits, had I not been greatly preoccupied by the reputation of Mélanie the Man-Tamer, without counting the cries of my publisher calling for more " copy. "

In wishing to see Mélanie, I was solely impelled by curiosity. Neither I nor you, reader, are " masochists. " At least, I am not, I assure you. Even if we were, we should not confess it, should we ?

Sadistic lechers, in a fit of frankness, at their ease among boon companions, might perhaps be cynical enough to confess that they like to slap a woman's bottom, or force her to obey their most exacting carnal caprices. " Masochists, " however, never confide the secret of their preferred pleasures. They cannot be avowed. Lovers of cruelty do not mind giving way to their passions in each other's company. I placed an example before you when telling of my escapade, Rue Clauzel. He who seeks to be a slave to the weaker sex is always alone with one or more women.

The little girl who is sitting on my knee, while she sips champagne out of my glass, as I caress her gently and perfidiously, giggles at my prolonged titillation, urging me to continue, adding :

"What a pity ! Fancy now—a nice, carefully

groomed chap like you, so jolly with a woman,
having such silly passions ! "

" What do you mean, my small sweetheart ? "

" Did you ask for big Mélanie, or not ? "

" Didn't know she was big ! But I do
want to see her—just to chat with her. That's
all ! "

" You fools of men all say the same thing,
and when she shows up, her fellow trembles
like a leaf, and follows her upstairs with his tail
between his legs ! "

" Where else would you have him carry it ? "
I interrupt, mockingly.

" Silly ! I can't make out what they all see
in her, or what fun they can have, considering
what she does to them all ! "

" What the deuce can she get up to ? Tell
me—there's a good girl ! "

" She don't do the same to everybody. Some
don't like all her ways. "

" What are they ? "

" I daresay you know—whipping, tying up,
pricking with pins and needles, making them

kiss or lick the carpet, or her feet—or worse !
Oh, I don't know ! And I don't much care !
Lots of other tricks too ! They make me
sick ! ''

She whispered some scatalogical revelations
in my astonished ear until I blushed for my
inverted fellow-men.

'' If you want to know any more, Mr. Inquisitive, you can ask Mélanie herself, for here
she comes ! ''

A tall woman, muscular and finely-built,
entered the room. She was very dark. Her
complexion was dead-white, but one could guess
that warm, healthy Southern blood coursed
freely beneath the ivory pallor of her skin.
Slight signs of black down shaded the upper
lip of her red, well-shaped mouth. She had
jet, bushy eyebrows, an aquiline nose, and her
forehead was low and narrow—betokening
obstinacy, if physiognomists are to be be-
lieved.

Her arms were superb, full and rounded,
with small wrists, swelling biceps, and dimpled
elbows. When she cared to throw open her dress-

inggown, which with a muslin chemise, stockings
and shoes, formed her sole garments, she showed
the small hard double glories of her bust. It
was the bosom of an Amazon—before mutila-
tion. Her legs were divinely modelled. She
had robust, swelling thighs, and the lower part
of her broad belly was amply garnished with
an inky fleece, meandering in three points, one
of which reached nearly up to her navel.

I cannot say that Mélanie is pretty, but she
is a fine, massive, living statue, capable of pro-
voking the desire of men who do not possess the
topsy-turvy feelings of her ordinary private
customers.

She looked at me with a frown rippling across
her forehead, and her eyelids, slightly wrinkled,
closing over her brilliant eyeballs in the mental
effort of trying to see if I was one of the weakly
sort she was used to, or whether I had ever been
with her before.

Seeing naught but curiosity in my frank
glance; finding that my voice betrayed no signs
of emotion when I begged her to accept a glass

of champagne, she was quite perplexed for a few seconds.

" Ah, I've got it ! " she exclaimed, guessing at the object of my visit at last. " You've come to ask me to tell you some stories ? "

" That's exactly what I want of you ! "

With rare good temper, she agreed to sit down and be interviewed without further ceremony.

" I like making fellows suffer. When a man is in pain, brought on when in my power, as I torture him by jealousy, humiliation, the rod or the whip, I feel a peculiar thrill run right through me. It's very nice—that feeling. I can't help it. It's not my fault. I expect I was born that way. I've always been rather cruel all my life. Although you mightn't think so, and it doesn't matter a straw to you—yet I'm proud to say that I'm a cut above common brothel bitches. I was well brought up and educated at a convent. A real convent—that surprises you, eh? I remember how I used to set traps for sparrows in the priory gardens. When I caught one, I always took the little bird in my hand and squeezed it slowly until the poor feathered thing was stifled. I had a strange sort of pleasure as I felt it trembling and panting in my grasp. As a young lass, I would play with lads of my own age, and when I could entice a boy into some lonely corner, I loved to slap, pinch, and kick him. My playfellows—gawky cubs they were!—did not seem to mind much, because they soon returned another day to romp with me again, putting up with my boxing their ears, scratching their faces and pulling their hair and noses, for the sake of the pleasures I granted them afterwards. "

" What induces a woman of your beauty and intelligence to remain in a brothel? "

" Because I have no risks or bother. Wherever I might go, my customers would always come and find me out. Here, I've no trouble of any kind. "

I kept on questioning her and she told me several stories of her slaves. Some of her reminiscences relating to masculine servitude were funny, so much so that they saddened me.

As I do not intend to let too much melancholy creep into these pages, I will not repeat her divulgations of the weaknesses of submissive mankind, and how she crushed her customers.

CHAPTER XII.

Students' Brothels.

The light-hearted amours of the Latin Quarter are celebrated all the world over. In this part of Paris, ardent youth breaks all barriers, and loves, learns and runs riot with the impetuosity of budding manhood.

As a natural consequence, arising from the loose manners and licence of the many young bachelors inhabiting this neighbourhood with no family ties to restrain them, authorised houses of ill-fame are not greatly honoured. The few second and third-rate brothels to be found on the left bank of the Seine are only frequented by students fresh from their homes in the country, or too silly and timid to sow their wild oats by the ordinary processes known to most young men.

If a young charmer, about fifteen or sixteen, of Montmartre or Belleville, is lucky enough to fall into the hands of some lad not too vile, although a pimp, he advises her to try life among the embryo lawyers and doctors. So she emigrates to some street near the Sorbonne, such as Rue Champollion, and lodges in a small room on the top floor of a furnished hotel.

She soon makes friends with a youth studying for the law, or walking the hospitals. If her apprentice sawbones or solicitor falls deeply in love with his companion, he takes her to live with him, and she becomes what is called an *étudiante*—female student. This is ironical. There is no danger of such a playful kitten being taken for one of those steady young women who really work side by side with male scholars— Russian girls, for instance.

In the case of an illicit union of this sort, the " ponce " goes growling back across the bridges. If he seeks for revenge, and makes too free with fist or knife, the police have to look after him, and he soon blossoms into the habitual criminal.

Trollops of all kinds muster in great force round the Panthéon and the Odéon Theatre. The Boulevard Saint Michel keeps up the tradition of ancient Lutetian merriment and gaiety.

At the present day, something may be seen in this brilliantly-lighted avenue that has almost disappeared from big Boulevards, such as the Boulevard des Italiens. At night, innumerable painted women are seated at tables outside the cafés. The sight reminds me of a row of butchers' stalls, so much meat being offered for sale in this slave-market.

The coming and going of these abandoned harlots with rustling skirts, bold manners and shrill laughter is most interesting to watch. Incessant gossiping, chaffering and haggling is heard, together with the choicest slang and most vile language. Highly comic scenes are enacted, delightful when witnessed by an unimpassioned and sober observer, while many a time and oft a battle of enraged trulls is waged. They pull each others's hair out by the roots, causing a crowd of passers-by to gather round the fighting strumpets.

Cocottes of the Quartier Latin are regular customers of the Café du Panthéon, or d'Harcourt, and the Brasserie Lorraine.

I find I am once more straying from my subject. The dolls I describe are in their houses. I must hie me back to my shut-up sluts. This is a book of brothels.

When the students of law, doctoring and art, are new to Paris, they either do not know the ropes or have not yet had time to pick up a sweetheart in the Luxembourg Garden, near the bandstand, when free open-air orchestral concerts are given. For such simple striplings, the brothels of their district are very useful, although these young men from the country prefer, as a rule, the cheap trollops and waitresses of the beershops lining the Rue de la Harpe and the Rue Monsieur-le-Prince.

The principal ready-money love temple of the students' quarter is familiarly called *La Botte de Paille*—"The Truss of Straw." It is in the Rue Mazarine, No. 49, close to the Rue de Buci. All lads installed in this part of the merry town to go through a course of education are forced by tradition to pay at least one visit to this quiet bagnio. If they refuse, they are unworthy, it is said, to style themselves Parisian students. Customs enforced by the unwritten laws of fashion are stupid. So is this one, for however gay a visitor may feel when stepping across the threshold of the Rue Mazarine hall of debauchery, he leaves it with feelings of the deepest sadness.

The saloon is reached from the street by a a narrow passage. Next comes a staircase, and lastly, a dull entrance-hall. The reception room is badly lighted, so that one can scarcely distinguish half-a-dozen, or so, of poor, soft-fleshed creatures, undeniably plain.

They advance reluctantly to be chosen by the client. The languid manner in which they present their meagre charms, or offer themselves to be carnally enjoyed, evokes ideas of sepulchral sensuality. They looked to me like ghosts of dead charmers allowed to revisit the earth for a night, receive the caresses of a man or two, and then return at cockcrow to their graves.

Some cynical Gallic moralist once affirmed that " marriage was the tomb of love. " He had never spent an hour at *La Botte de Paille.*

The next brothel in these parts, No. 5, Rue des Quatre-Vents, is a trifle better so far as fittings and decoration are concerned.

The boarders are also morose young misses, anæmic and faded. Nevertheless, should you take the trouble to chat with them a little, and ask them questions, they all declare that they are of excellent parentage.

" My father was a Colonel, " is generally the opening falsehood of their confession. " He used to be invited to the Palace of the Tuileries before the war ! You don't seem to be very randy to-night, dear boy ? The Emperor was particularly fond of him— why won't it stand? —and as for the Empress, she always—you've been drinking too much beer perhaps ?—liked him to accompany her when she—feel my breasts while I caress you ; that'll warm you up perhaps—went out driving," etc.

If these aristocratic memories of the Second

Empire do not arouse your hidden fires of
lubricity, you are surely hopelessly impotent.

By some inexplicable topographical caprice,
the real brothel of the students is situated on
the right bank of the Seine, and the rising gene-
ration crosses the water to revel in the delights
of No. 37, Rue des Petits-Carreaux.

As years roll on, the students of Paris frequent brothels less than ever. A visit to cloistered harlots is an untoward incident in the
amorous career of a future attorney or surgeon.
It may happen that his companion, *l'étudiante*,
is tired ; fagged out through having stopped up
several nights, drinking, dancing and skylarking
in the company of her lover and his chums.
The spree is generally carried on by a band of
joyous couples and odd solitary youths, when
boyish laughter and girlish song continue from
dinner to dawn. Next day, the girl-concubine
refuses her adorer's advances. He seeks satisfaction elsewhere. He also becomes unfaithful when the dates of the almanack remind his
mistress of the periodical suffering peculiar to
her sex.

At such times, the little woman, each year of her life, "thirteen times unclean," as the French poet hath it, chastely drops her eyes, whispering to her own darling boy:

"Go out to-night, doggie pet, if you like! Go to the Rue des Petits-Carreaux and *have your pen cut*. I'll allow you—for once in a way, because pussy's poorly!"

Tailler une plume is the slang expression I have literally translated. It signifies the act of labial pollution, when a man sullies the rosy mouth and lips of a consenting female.

This enervating caress is the *summum bonum* of Parisian debauchees. It is most common in literary circles. Brain-workers have constant recourse to this violent refinement of lewd enjoyment, being passionately fond of it.

Constant abuse of this kind, however, produces results analogous to the absinthe habit, inevitably destroying intellectual power, acting fatally on the spinal marrow, bringing about degenerescence of the grey matter and locomotor ataxy.

Despite these terrible consequences, Frenchmen adore the sweet prolonged agony of submitting lazily to the terrible genital excitement induced by the voluptuous toying of a mistress's warm, velvety lips and tongue. As scholars and writers prefer this selfish style of spasm, the expression of " pen cutting" is most appropriate. This sensual slang is, for a wonder, decently worded, and can be used in the presence of the most innocent maidens or children. The initiated votaries of Venus close their eyes and call up tantalising visions of oral congress at once, dreaming of the melting mouth and its insidious, soft contact.

Obedient to the farewell commands of his sweetheart, the student sets out. His own girl has permitted him to gorge his youthful sex-hunger with this infamous caress, because she does not consider that her darling little man is unfaithful to her if he allows a venal anonymous brothel toy to provoke his orgasm in such decadent fashion. She has told him to repair to the house of harlots in the Rue des Petits-Carreaux, because she has been told that its girls are healthy and clean.

The young man strolls through the streets. He hesitates. His unwonted liberty is not half so enjoyable as he thought it was going to be. He flourishes his stick—students love to carry heavy cudgels—threateningly ; then deals a blow with his fist on the top of his soft felt hat. This pantomime of exasperation denotes that he is saying to himself, " I'm a free man ! I'm not going to be ordered about by a bit of a girl ! Not I ! "

Instead of wending his way over the water to the right bank of the Seine, he remains in the lively Latin Quarter, and stalks briskly to the Rue des Feuillantines, where there is also a very ordinary house of debauchery for lustful lads.

He goes in and is disappointed. The strumpets on view are shockingly unattractive. He repents having disobeyed his mistress's orders, and winds up where he ought to have begun—at the Rue des Petits-Carreaux.

Again I have to note a long, narrow entry and the ascent of a staircase, when the ordinary door of Parisian flats confronts the seeker of fornication. Our student touches the button of an electric bell, and is admitted by a polite housekeeper.

She conducts him to a neat little drawing-room where the walls are simply covered with ruby-coloured flock paper.

The bawdy regiment troops in, and, dazzled by the sight of so much savoury flesh, he tries to keep cool and pass in review a most delicious group of vestals.

It seems incredible that even in Paris, the city of sensuous miracles, a man may enjoy such fine females for the paltry sum of five francs—four shillings, one dollar ! For this bit of silver, the supreme voluptuous caress I have just mentioned is bestowed with loving care.

Should you choose Diane, a superb blonde, a real, plump Rubens ; or be struck by the dashing, proud grace of Ernestine, a lively brunette, you will be kissed into Paradise in the most painstaking, slowly-scientific manner. They know how to operate. And yet people dare to say that Paris is an expensive city !

The " fellatrice " has always been greatly sought after in the French capital. Some twenty years ago, a lady specialist in the art of " cutting pens " made a fortune by her infamous kissing. She has departed this world.

Her name was Angèle Bardin, but she called herself Baronne d'Ange. She was also known as *la honte de Paris*. She was ugly at her zenith, forty years of age, at least, although I have been told that as a young woman she was possessed of considerable comeliness. She was endowed with unblushing effrontery, advertising herself by her love of horseflesh. Every day she drove up the Avenue des Champs-Elysées, round the Bois de Boulogne and home again to the Rue Saint-Georges, where she had a private house of her own. She tooled a splendid pair, a silver crossbar surmounting the stately withers of her prancing steeds. By her side, sat her husband, a most insignifiant person who seemed rather bored by the impudent stare of the passers-by.

This remarkable prostitute was reputed to be a perfect wonder when it came to kneeling before her innumerable visitors. She was notorious for her salacious talent, which proved the source of a great fortune, although her price never varied. She effected her purpose in five minutes, and received twenty francs; sometimes being satisfied with half that amount, if her friend of a moment did not take up too much of her time.

Amateurs of this artificial joy beseiged her dwelling, and it has been gravely stated that she had to fit up separate stalls, or loose-boxes, so to speak, like the little glazed trying-on compartments at tailor's shops, where her clients waited their turn. No fashionable doctor or dentist ever had such a procession of customers. It is true that professors of healing arts charge higher fees, and instead of dealing out doses of delight, their prices increase in proportion to the degree of pain they inflict.

Forty or fifty men passed through her hands—I use this expression out of politeness—in the course of the day, and she "worked" from ten till noon, two to four, and from eight

to ten. She had a younger woman with her—
a sort of obliging assistant—but most visitors,
allured by her world-wide fame, came to
submit to the ghoulish efforts of the mistress of
the house. Before beginning her vampire play,
which took place in a dimly-lighted room, her
willing victim was asked to stretch himself on a
sofa. The priestess of the palace of irruma-
tion then deigned with her own fair hands to
perform certain private ablutions, using rose-
water.

In the centre of the elegant drawing-room,
stood a fountain with a jet of water always mer-
rily splashing. Rumours were current at the
time of the Baronne d'Ange's greatest vogue
concerning the gold-fish swimming in the marble
basin. It was said they were exceptionally fat
and in grand condition. I can only say that
when I sampled the skill of the so-called Baron-
ess, I did not notice these piscatorial prodigies,
although handy Angèle did expectorate into
the fountain.

Another legend ascribes the invention of the
now common phrase, *tailler une plume*, to

her, because she found so many men of letters
seeking her sofa in order to savour the gradual
relief of her renowed sensual speciality.   I do
not think she was witty enough, but probably
the "pen-cutting" joke was suggested by one or
the other of the clever pressmen who paid her to
practise her art upon their throbbing persons.

The foregoing digression simply leads me to
the conclusion that for a modest five-franc piece,
the student finds at the Petits-Carreaux bagnio
that the secrets of the Baronne d'Ange are fully
known to its beauteous boarders. They are
quite as clever as defunct Angèle Bardin, and
eminently superior to her from an æsthetical
point of view, being young and pretty.

The brothel of the Rue des Petits-Carreaux
formerly occupied but one story, but it has
been re-decorated, embellished, and extended
by the adjunction of the flat above.

Some twelve years ago it was famous as being
the main resort for "lookers-on"—in French,
voyeurs—lechers, who without being seen
themselves, love to view couples sacrificing to
Venus. To satisfy gentleman with the tastes

of Peeping Tom, holes were drilled in the walls, or glazed doors were arranged in the partitions, and soon nearly every room in the place had a spy-hole concealed in the hangings.

I remember going myself. I said, " I come to *see* ! " A saucy little brunette, named Marthe, accompanied me. She took me into the kitchen. Concealed by a bright copper saucepan hanging on the wall was a small aperture pierced in the plaster, through which an adjoining bedroom could be seen—and its fornicating occupants as well.

A looking-on epidemic seemed to be hovering over Paris, and many other bawdy-houses copied the Petits-Carreaux peep-show.

Some of the palpitating puppets I looked upon knew they were being seen and liked the idea. Marthe once asked me if I cared to peep at a man who had asked to be looked at. I consented, and saw a sturdy naked fellow whose head was wrapped round with an antimacassar of crochet work. He could see and breathe, but his features were quite unrecognisable as he posed, strutted and attitudinised while toying with one of the wantons of the place. The masked man was evidently delighted at being admired while he played at being a very shameless satyr.

At last, these looking-on sports formed the talk of the town at the Bourse and at every club. Scandal was rife, so the police stepped in and stopped up all the indiscreet orifices.

Marthe of the Petits-Carreaux was a buxom amiable lass. While I peeped, she would remain by my side to kiss and caress me, exciting me physically, while the salacious spectacle thrilled me mentally. I often wondered how my gentle guide managed to maintain the firmness of her big breasts. She afterwards became directress of the Petits-Carreaux brothel, having thus worked her way up from the ranks to the post of commanderess-in-chief.

CHAPTER XIII.

Round the Halles.

Zola called the Halles—the Central Markets
—the "Ventre de Paris." He was right. In
these vast sheds of glass and iron, full of busy
people, is concentrated the essence of Parisian
life : hard work and love of pleasure.

The Lutetian Central Markets never sleep ;
they teem with life incessantly. Day breaks
and the high-livers who have sought this neighbourhood to sup in one of its numerous all-
night restaurants crawl home to bed. As they
depart, great carts full of vegetables from the
suburbs or food-stuffs from the railway stations,
thunder in to discharge their heavy loads.

The quarrelsome lads of Montmartre and

Belleville meet here with the boys of Mont-
rouge, to drink, and more often to fight with
knives and revolvers. The perfumed courtesans and their keepers in full evening dress,
who, in the small hours, enjoy the cunning
cookery at Baratte's, the best supper-room in
these parts, are sometimes startled by distant
pistol-shots.

The habitual frequenters of the "Ange
Gabriel" wineshop, in the Rue Pirouette, are
settling some little private matter, always relating to loving rivalry. A woman is at the
bottom of all mischief!

Sometimes sweet modern Helen reveals
her presence by a loud shriek of agony. She
howls with fright and pain, a great dagger
sticking in her dimpled back, between her two
shoulders.

There are other curious dangerous dens of
this kind round about here. The "Caveau,"
full of pimps and streetwalkers; the restaurant
of the "Chien qui fume," where cluster pretty
living "lay-figures," from the fashionable dressmakers, and bejewelled swell "molls," from

the best parts of the town. The "Sébasto" —Boulevard de Sébastopol—is close by, with its river of prostitutes, rolling, ebbing and flowing, brimming over into adjacent streets.

All these shady haunts of the seamy side of Paris have only a slight connection with my subject. I merely quote a few of them to let my reader judge the character of the quarter, and then I ask him to kindly follow me to the Rue Blondel, which reaches from the Rue Saint Denis and the Rue Saint Martin, cutting across the beginning of the "Sébasto."

This narrow lane can boast of five licensed houses—all very ordinary. From time to time, notwithstanding, something uncommon may be picked up in them. The habitual client of these prosaic knocking-shops is not sufficiently refined to appreciate any woman unless she be of a common type. The pigs of Paris disdain a priceless pearl, half hidden in the refuse of the carnal city.

It happened thus with Zulma. She was a tall, bronzed lass from Kabylia, on the far frontiers of Algeria, and was only seventeen, but she carried a forged certificate of birth, showing that she had come of age. Speaking French tolerably well, she had travelled all alone from Algiers to Paris where she hoped to make her fortune. When she stepped out of the train, she held tightly clasped in her little brown fist, a scrap of paper on which was scribbled in pencil the address of the licensed brothel, No. 57, Rue Blondel.

Lithe, slender and graceful, but without a bone or a rib to be seen, her amber skin was always cool to the touch. Her eyes were the biggest black orbs I have ever seen ; their velvet caressing glance was feverishly brilliant, giving the impression of a stormy summer sky when leaden stillness warns us of the coming tempest. Zulma would look at her man calmly, with great assurance, and her quiet stare thrilled the customer through and through. The boldness of her glances contrasted strangely with the pure contours of her features and her delicate profile of classic regularity.

She was a weird lass. Compared to Parisian trulls, she was thin, and the lechers of this neighbourhood want something plump for their money. They like to find good handfuls to mould and press in the lace of the chemise, and trouble little about the quality of the flesh as long as there is lots of it.

The slim, serpentine beauty of half-savage Zulma; her long legs and arms; small wrists and ankles, but exquisitely-rounded all the same, did not appeal to their senses. Their ideal of a fine woman is a coarse and massive wet-nurse.

Moreover, the darling of the desert took no pains to entice a customer. She did nothing but dart her unfathomable, undefinable glance into his eyes. If the charm of her lustrous pupils produced its effect, the man was hypnotised, and experienced rare, bizarre pleasure in her arms.

This peculiar girl's kisses were dry and hard, spiced with a monstrous perfume, like that exhaled by certain orchids. It was a scent of peculiar softness, and so sweet that it seemed to provoke a feeling of delicious faintness, being more subtle and penetrating than musk.

Zulma's lips and tongue, with their fragrant odour, gave caresses that were deliciously cool, and yet this refreshing touch of her pink mouth produced an after-glow of heat that sent a line of flame along the spine.

Her preliminary toying was nothing in comparison to the delight experienced when she was fully enjoyed. Those long arms and lissom legs; the whole of her tall, sweet frame, glistening like burnished metal, possessing the strength and suppleness of tropical creeping plants or of serpents, fastened itself to her partner. Her lover of the hour was enwrapped, lost, so to say, in the clinging bondage of those tepid limbs.

With Zulma, I have felt myself as if captive, bound hand and foot, powerless to do aught but desire her madly. Then a feeling almost like torture, caused an upheaval of my whole being, as the ardour of her sex scorched me with its fierce fire. The sensation, when my virility had been absorbed in her, was as if I were slipping into a furnace. It was inexpressibly delicious.

This child of Nature, more civilised than the Parisians, only knew how to give herself up to the male in ordinary fashion. She rebelled against the salacious whims of bawdy-house Don Juans, and being neglected, made no money. So one fine day, she was suddenly dismissed without notice.

Zulma's few assiduous clients who appreciated the sublime simplicity of her enlacing spell, were well-nigh crazy when they came to sate their desire and found her not.

One of these gentlemen, a rich tradesman of the quarter, travelled expressly to Algeria to find her, after having scoured Paris. Half the money he spent in useless search would have sufficed to take the siren of the Sahara from the lowly lupanar, set her up in a small lodging and keep her for some time.

There is nothing in the Rue Blondel for me to describe, so I step round to the Rue d'Aboukir, where at the cloistered homes of copulation, Nos. 161 and 131, I remark the same absence of beauty as I mentioned before. The girls are below the standard, barely good enough to satisfy the cravings of the young assistants from the wholesale drapers of the vicinity. These youths have more illusions than cash, and therefore are not fastidious.

This Rue d'Aboukir is full of furnished hotels where dwell prostitutes whose speciality consists in enticing men to rob them. These brigand-whores work in couples. While one smothers her client with moist kisses, and lewdly provokes lascivious pleasure, the other searches in the pockets of the fellow's garments thrown over the back of a chair, or the foot of the bed.

A step farther, and I find myself in the Rue Sainte-Foy, where there are three most uninteresting brothels.

The sluts of these shuttered stews are old and ugly. These houses are devoted to pauper prostitution which can be studied elsewhere, as I will try to demonstrate in my next chapter.

So I leave the Rue Sainte-Foy, and beg you, reader, to come with me to Grenelle. It is a long way from where we are now, but you have only to turn to the following page.

CHAPTER XIV.

At Grenelle.

Among the decrepit elderly prostitutes who walk the streets round about the column of the Bastille, towards Charenton; on the Morgue bridge; in the vicinity of the Place Maubert; or even on the fortifications between the Rue du Poteau and the Rue des Rosiers at Saint Ouen, there may sometimes be seen a young and pretty girl. When found, it is certain she will be in rags. But beauty always carries the day, and the fresh, plump allurement of a young unused body is remarkable, even when it is that of Venus unwashed.

Some rakes like to try conclusions with these uncivilised ragpickers' daughters, who know nothing about soap and water. I have heard

of an authentic prince, allied to a reigning family
of Europe, who had a mania for making the
acquaintance of fifteen-year-old hussies. He
always told his procuresses and purveyors to
bring the minxes to him as they were found,
without forcing them to have a bath.

He sought for the *odor di femina*, and generally got it—to the full. If his beloved perfume was absent, he would exclaim with a sigh:
" They've been bathing this girl again, and
they've spoilt her entirely! "

At Grenelle, there is not the slightest chance
of finding any youthful harlots. In this part
of Paris, pauper prostitution alone exists, in
plain squalid horror. The soldiers of the
neighbouring barracks have to be satisfied with
these hags.

The street-walkers of the Boulevard Gari-
baldi and the Boulevard de Grenelle are generally between forty and seventy. In the Rue
Frémicourt and the Rue Letellier, nearly every
other house is a miserable *café* where dreadfully ugly and repulsively dirty waitresses try
to entice a customer into dark little back pre-

mises. Once there, they work hard to tempt him to go upstairs with them to a bedroom, and revel in their crumbling charms, which they gladly abandon for one franc.

On the Boulevard de Grenelle, close to the Rue Frémicourt, is a brothel. There are many in this neighbourhood, but I choose this one because it is a typical specimen, giving a sufficient idea of all the others.

The decaying old building has a low frontage. I enter a saloon on the basement, flush with the street. I can almost touch the ceiling with my head. Two or three naked gas-jets are flaring in an atmosphere of rank dust and stale tobacco. About ten women await clients. Some of them, with the inherent laziness peculiar to lupanar lasses, loll or recline at full length on a bench covered with dirty velvet; the rest are trying to tell each other's fortune with a greasy pack of well-worn cards.

My apparition causes a flutter of excitement. These unfortunates are more used to seeing carters, masons, and privates of line regiments than well-dressed men of the middle classes.

Nevertheless, there exist in Paris a few habitual frequenters of such stews as these, gentlemen with topsy-turvy tastes whose sensual feelings are increased tenfold by sordid surroundings. They cannot pour out their libation on the altar of Venus unless their female companion in the whirl of lubricity is a filthy harridan. Maniacs of this species pay indigent harlots as generously as if they sported old lace and cambric, or wore pearl necklaces round perfumed necks.

Two ladies come smirking towards me, offering their bodies with antiquated awkward grace. It is impossible to conceive greater ugliness.

One of them makes determinedly for me. She is hideously fat. Despite her obesity, she wears a short petticoat, hardly reaching to her knees, so that I have a full view of a pair of legs like those of an elephant, massive and shapeless. Her attenuated skirt makes this obese old woman look bigger still. She must be fifty at least, and glances at me in a strange confused way, being so short-sighted that she knocks her nose against her wine-glass. I have been foolish enough to offer her some refreshment.

Seated with her, I examine her eyes closely, noticing the pupils are covered with whitish spots. The poor creature suffers from amaurosis.

Notwithstanding heavy drooping cheeks, and many hanging chins, her features betray remains of delicate regularity, persisting in spite of the invasion of adipose tissue.

There is not the slightest doubt that the antique ruin by my side was formerly a most beautiful woman. After I have been chatting with her five minutes, I find that she reveals herself as a lady, full of wit and tact. Her manners are those of one used to good society, and it is evident she is entirely out of her element in this lowest circle of the purgatory of Parisian prostitution.

Am I in the company of a duchess? Most decidedly not, but this senile siren has belonged to the few high-class courtesans who, in their turn, are the despotic queens of rich, money-burning libertines; heroines of a thousand adventures, of whom the whole city gossips, wanting to know all about their dresses, jewels and countless caprices; the daughters of our desire, who like Circe, change men into swine, break the hearts of their numerous slavish adorers, and melt their fortunes in the ardent crucible of the most fatal love.

"You're a cut above this wretched place," I tell my companion. "I've seen you before in better circumstances—that I'll swear! Tell me who you are?"

She giggles and changes the subject. Knowing women's ways, I bide my time and talk of something else. I feel that what I have said will sink into her brain, and if I am right, the answer to my query will come later. As I expected, she harks back of her own accord, whispers a name in my ear, and bursts out laughing.

"What I've told you doesn't make me look younger, eh? Now you know my secret, I don't mind confessing that I'm fifty-seven, my dear fellow. And now, can't I tempt you to spend a short hour with me? Who knows? Perhaps you won't repent it! You never can tell, you know!"

Conquering a momentary feeling of repulsion, I consent, actuated partly by pity and partly by a wish to acquire information that may serve for my notes. Could I hope for a more precious guide in the labyrinth of Parisian prostitution, past and present?

Although I accepted her offer to retire from public view with her, still I knew that my thirst for knowledge would not overpower my physical repugnance. I resolved to refuse the consummation of "the act." I was sure that if I declined her proposition of copulation firmly and politely, the poor woman would be too delicate to insist.

I followed her up a tortuous staircase, and through dark and stifling narrow corridors, we at last reached a small room with the ceiling on our heads.

Unfortunately for me, she tried to play her part seriously, refusing to accept the platonic position I had destined for her. It was pitiful to see how she tried to blend her courtesy of bygone days with the vile necessities of her present situation.

She was profuse in her excuses for not being able to offer me the resources of a dressing-room, and with a laugh, extracted a basin from a small, mirrored wardrobe.

" It is not of regulation size or shape, but it is my bidet nevertheless! " she exclaimed, pressing me to make use of it.

I tried to make her see that I only wanted to interview her, but she did not or would not understand, and it was all I could do to get away from this female ruin.

When I reached the ground-floor, she acknowledged my farewell salutations with the haughty bearing of an outraged princess.

As I stepped out in the night, and drew a long breath of sweet, pure air, I asked myself if after all, this deplorable hag was really lovely Léonie de Closménil, for whom, about twenty-five years ago, an Austrian prince spent much money, and behaved so foolishly that his family had him shut up in a madhouse. " La

Belle Bouchère," as she was called, being the daughter of a dealer in fresh meat at Bordeaux, betrayed her spendthrift archduke every day with her coachman, but she did not forget, between whiles, to pluck other pigeons. I remember hearing of a great sugar-refiner who showered gold upon her. Really I can write no more. It is too sad to think of the terrible fate of a former queen of Parisian pleasure.

It would be easy to philosophise with trite and hackneyed sentences, were it not that this modern harlot's progress points its own moral.

CHAPTER XV.

A Common Error. — "Lookers-On." Socratic Love.

———

A Parisian affects great scepticism, but his apparent pessimism hides an ingenuous and credulous soul.

He believes implicitly in the legend of "lookers-on," and nearly always when visiting a brothel, before allowing his chosen charmer to clasp him in her mercenary arms, runs round the room, scrutinising and tapping at the walls, lifting up curtains, peering behind pictures and mirrors, concluding by going down on his knees to glare under the bed.

He is suffering from the "looking-on" obsession, a besetting idea firmly rooted in his brain. He is convinced that at most licensed houses of lewdness, in return for large sums of money, *voyeurs* are allowed to assist at the customers' fornicating frolics, so that they may gloat over the voluptuous coition of unsuspecting citizens with the girls of the bagnio. Every wall is pierced with holes; all looking-glasses are hung up in such a way that they throw reflexions of beds and sofas towards the hidden orifice where the concealed witness darts his fiery concupiscent eye upon the games of sex—a most enchanting sight for the amateur afflicted with this inquisitorial mania for poking his nose into other people's bawdy business.

Nothing of the kind exists at present. Any house of municipal eroticism where such lascivious spying was permitted would be immediately closed by order of the police. No proprietor of an establishment of licensed prostitution would risk having his business brought to a sudden and ruinous close for the sake of the small extra profits such obliging traffic would bring in.

It is quite certain that at the first-class houses I have tried to describe—Rue Chabanais,

Rue Montyon, and Rue Joubert, there are no *voyeurs* nowadays, except by permission of all parties concerned.

I have told how a couple in coition can be seen Rue de Londres. There, I shrewdly suspect that the acting and active male is an accomplice, a mere paid actor, perfectly cognisant that he is being looked at by concealed witnesses.

I have been told that in the Rue Grange-Batelière there exists a brothel where peripatetic prostitutes prowling up and down the Faubourg Montmartre take their victims enticed in the streets. These nymphs of the pavement know that amateurs, their mouths watering with expectant salacity, are in ambush to watch the combat of the couple on the battlefield of Venus.

In the vicinity of the Etoile triumphal arch, near the Avenue de l'Alma, and also in the Avenue Wagram, there are houses—generally wretched furnished hotels—where boys with painted faces are at the disposal of depraved individuals with sodomical tastes. These places of meeting for pederastic inverts are generally run by catamites, who, having become too old and ugly to sell their own vile bodies, traffic in those of others, exactly as the decrepit elderly trollop becomes a procuress.

There used to be a lodging-house of this kind in the Rue d'Aboukir, and as I write, I hear of a hotel in the Rue Saint Martin. It has just been raided and its owner condemned to eighteen months' imprisonment for having exploited several lads of tender age. He treated them like a slave-driver, or an Italian *padrone*, driving gutter-boys with rouged cheeks and blackened eyelashes out on the Boulevards to bring back wealthy amateurs of sodomitical lust to his stuffy bedrooms.

These wretched mercenary young fellows are sent for by bawdy-house keepers when a customer with cash wishes to enjoy an erotic scene.

I am not, however, writing about pederastic Paris, and only quote these instances so far as they touch upon the brothel industry.

To be exact, I must not forget to mention

that there is a colony of these misguided youths in the district of the Panthéon. There are many in the Rue Saint-Jacques.

In the latter street, almost at the angle of the Rue Soufflot, I had been hospitably received by a charming lady. It was a summer's night.

About one o'clock in the morning, I heard cries and groans.

" No! no! I'll not do it! " exclaimed a man, with tears and sobs.

" Yes, sir, you will! You must! " replied a calm, musical, masculine voice.

Then there was more talking, moaning, and outbursts of laughter.

I rose and went to the window. Looking out, I saw, at the corner of the street, a group of young fellows, who, by their eccentric, effeminate garb, were doubtless male prostitutes, surrounding a fine-looking, aristocratic young man. The latter had nothing on but his shirt.

The band of sodomites pushed him about, and hustled him, each in their turn. One of the simpering degenerates acted as ringleader, commanding the half-nude victim to execute most extraordinary penances.

He had to lick the pavement, drink out of the gutter, and was told to run round a public urinal, where finally the captain of the crapulous crew went in with him.

What took place in the shelter of the little edifice, I know not, but when the young gentleman in his shirt reappeared, he put on his clothes, which were lying in a heap on the ground, and got into a natty brougham, awaiting his orders. On the box sat the coachman, impassible, staring abstractedly straight before him. He whipped up his horse and drove off. After a parting chorus of mocking jeers, the painted men-harlots hurried away.

THE END.

ORDER FORM
Attach a separate sheet for additional titles.

Title   Quantity   Price

_____ ___ _____

_____ ___ _____

_____ ___ _____

_____ ___ _____

Shipping and Handling (see charges below) _____

Sales tax (in CA and NY) _____

Total _____

Name _____

Address _____

City _____ State _____ Zip _____

Daytime telephone number _____

❏ Check   ❏ Money Order   (US dollars only. No COD orders accepted.)

Credit Card # _____ Exp. Date _____

❏ MC   ❏ VISA   ❏ AMEX

Signature _____

(if paying with a credit card you must sign this form.)

Shipping and Handling charges:*

Domestic: $4 for 1st book, $.75 each additional book. International: $5 for 1st book, $1 each additional book
*rates in effect at time of publication. Subject to Change.

Mail order to Publishers Group West, Attention: Order Dept., 1700 Fourth St., Berkeley, CA 94710,
or fax to (510) 528-3444.

PLEASE ALLOW 4-6 WEEKS FOR DELIVERY. ALL ORDERS SHIP VIA 4TH CLASS MAIL.

Look for Blue Moon Books at your favorite local bookseller
or from your favorite online bookseller.